REignited

REignited

LOVE'S WORTH SERIES #2
A NOVELLA

Published by
TWO REALMS PUBLISHING LLC
HTTPS://TWO-REALMS-PUBLISHING-LLC.COM/
ISBN: 978-1-955106-17-7

Cover and Interior Design: We Got You Covered Book Design

TWOREALMS
PUBLISHING

Printed in the United States of America

REignited

LOVE'S WORTH SERIES
BOOK TWO

BRIGIT ROSÉ

To my fans!

*For being super supportive and extra patient
with me while I finished this bad boy.*

one

CLUTCHING THE GRAY JUMPSUIT, EZZIE stopped in front of the desk to complete processing. It was more like a ticket booth than a desk, one that was connected to a small room. It might seem as if being inside the tiny box would be worse than being on the outside. Except the person on the inside hadn't been arrested. Unlike her, they hadn't spent a night in jail. It was definitely worse on the outside. At least she was back in her own clothes and getting out.

For now.

She opened the metal drawer, placed the gray jumpsuit inside of it and shoved it back in place.

"Go to the door on your left and wait for the buzzer. You'll collect the rest of your things on the other side," a gruff voice said.

"Okay." Turning to her left, Ezzie headed down the short hallway toward the exit. Crikey, she couldn't wait to get out of there. Her sneakers squeaked against the black and white, checkered linoleum floor. She waited in front of the door as instructed until she heard the buzzer, then she pushed on the door and stepped into another room.

At least this one was bigger than the previous one. If she was lucky, it would be the last. She glanced to the woman at the desk to her right. It was an actual desk. Just a tall wooden frame. No glass on top or window to speak through. No drawer for the collection of items. Blessed freedom had to be around the corner.

"Name?" the woman behind the desk squawked.

"Esmeralda Donovan."

"Date of birth?"

As if there was another person running around town with the same name. Ezzie frowned. If that had been the case, she could claim mistaken identity. Innocent was a hell of a lot better.

"April 30, 1997."

A gray-haired woman with no smile placed a plastic bag atop the desk alongside a clipboard with a paper attached to it. "Sign here."

Again, she followed the instructions given. She hadn't had to worry about anything so specific since her first year of college. Even her recipes didn't require exact measurements. If the flour was a little less than cup, no big deal. If the sugar tipped a touch over three tablespoons, so what. Not here. Ezzie did precisely what she'd been told. With her signature complete, she collected the bag and removed her belongings: cell phone, wallet, and keys.

"You're free to go, Miss Donovan. Head down that hallway there." The woman gestured to an empty hall behind the desk.

"Thank you."

Best news she'd heard in the last twenty-four hours. Ezzie walked in the direction the officer pointed out. She marched down the corridor, which lead into a large room bustling with movement. From those going through metal detectors to the people exiting, there was so much going on it made her departure that much more inconspicuous. Not as if she'd really be noticed by anyone that mattered or knew her. Thank god for small favors. News of her arrest would get around soon enough, and the longer it took, the longer her reputation remained intact.

Of all the places she never thought she'd wind up strolling out of, a police station was definitely on that list. Ezzie stepped through the glass doors and into the warm sun. There was no time to focus on that. Scanning the cars parked along the sidewalk, she spotted her best friend's blue sedan and started down the cement staircase.

She climbed into the passenger side of the car. "Thanks for getting me, Matt."

"*And* bailing you out. Speaking of, do you have any idea what you were arrested for?"

"Thank you for that. And yes, but it's ridiculous."

Did they have to talk about it right then? All she wanted to do at that moment was get home so she could hug her son. Then she could worry about getting them on a plane to Utah. She needed help and there was only one person she could turn to: her brother. Nate was a lawyer and this was a case that would be right up his alley.

She hadn't been home in nearly five years.

If there had ever been a reason to go back, this was definitely it.

"We, the jury, find the defendant ... not guilty," said the foreman.

Yes! Luke thought. He couldn't always tell which way a jury would go in these cases, although his gut had yet to steer him wrong. Still, he liked it when he was proven right.

His client turned toward him and held out her hand. "Thank you so much for everything, Mr. Jonnihan."

"You're quite welcome, Ms. Jacobson. Happy to be of service." He shook her hand.

Maintaining her hold on his hand, she swept her blonde hair over her shoulder. "I'd love to buy you a drink in celebration of the verdict."

Have mercy. Do I have something stamped on my forehead that reads please flirt with me? The last thing he wanted was a woman in his life. He had his work and his new firm. That was enough to fulfill him. Sure, he might desire a special someone and a family one day, but he had plenty of time.

Besides, he hadn't exactly found anyone who'd been able to measure up to his expectations. He hadn't really been looking recently either, and even if he *had* been searching, his client didn't fit the bill.

"I appreciate the offer, but I really should get back to the office."

"Suit yourself." Releasing his hand, she grinned and sauntered down the gallery aisle.

Cracking his neck, Luke dragged a hand down his face and packed up his briefcase. He really had to stop taking on female clients. Most of them hit on him, even the two who were married. Maybe he just needed to find an inexpensive wedding ring to wear around clients, although, they might ask questions about his non-existent wife. He grabbed the handle of his briefcase, strode down the gallery aisle and exited the courtroom.

There was no good solution.

He refused to risk his and Nate's firm because women asked for non-billable time. And he couldn't fake a marriage just to keep them from flirting. The front pocket of his suit jacket vibrated. Luke dug out his cell phone and glanced at the caller before answering it. "Hi, Nate."

"What's the verdict?"

"Not guilty on all charges."

Another win for the firm. They may have only graduated and passed the bar a couple of years ago, but they'd built a strong reputation for their firm in the last six months. It had been risky for them to go into business together so soon after their graduation, but they each had stable reputations on the circuit to put into their own firm. And it had always been the plan.

"That's awesome, man! Woo! We're on fire!"

All they had to do was keep the momentum going. One bad case or wrong move could set back everything they'd strived to accomplish. Not something he could have happen, especially since their firm was all he had. All he'd likely have. He couldn't think about that right then.

"We're doing good. How's everything with your theft case going?"

"Howard texted me earlier that he found a video we might be interested in. He's bringing it by the office first thing tomorrow morning."

"Excellent. I'm heading to the office now if he wants to come by sooner." Finalizing everything on this last case could probably wait until tomorrow, but he planned to get it done while it was all fresh in his mind. He hated putting things off.

"Seriously? Luke, come on, man. Go out and celebrate the win or go home and relax. The paperwork isn't going anywhere."

Luke unlocked his BMW and climbed in the driver side. Setting his briefcase in the passenger seat, he shifted the phone and shut the door. "This is how I celebrate."

"Didn't you used to go out with the guys from your last firm after a win?"

"Only once or twice."

They'd hung out a few times, but it only made him crave time by himself. Half of them talked about their wives and/or girlfriends and the other half talked about all the women they intended to bang over the weekend. Either way, it only reminded him of one person— the one person he didn't want to think about.

"All right. Do what you want, man. Just don't forget about my parent's anniversary party this weekend. You're expected to be there."

Of course he was; it had been that way for the last few years. The first couple of years he'd made up excuses. He hadn't been all that prepared to run into Ezzie. At least until he discovered she hadn't attended either. After that, he made it a point to be there. Not that she ever showed up. He didn't anticipate her presence this year either.

"You know I will be."

"Good. I'll talk to you later."

"Sure thing."

Luke hung up and tucked his cell phone back into the front pocket of his jacket. Ezzie had been the last person he wanted to think about. He rubbed his eyes, turned the ignition, and the engine roared to life. The office was definitely the right decision.

It was the one place that could distract him from all the things he didn't want to feel.

And it was certainly better than getting drunk.

Ezzie popped the can of cherry Dr. Pepper open and poured it into the mix of flour and cocoa powder. Setting the can of pop aside, she picked up a wooden spoon and stirred the mixture. Her cherry chocolate-chip cupcakes would be the perfect dessert for later. Thankfully, the party for her parents' anniversary celebration wasn't until tomorrow. It gave her time to talk to her brother about her situation with her son peacefully passed out in her room, which was exactly why she was preparing her son's favorite dessert.

He didn't need to overhear anything, especially since she kind of figured her brother would freak out a little bit. Okay, a lot. Probably about as much as she had when the police had shown up to her bakery, arrested her, and escorted her away in handcuffs. Maybe she should wait until after her parents' anniversary party to talk to him.

No, it's too urgent to put off; it has to be tonight, Ezzie thought. Her and her son's future were at stake.

They had to come up with a plan, one that would keep her out of jail.

The side door to the kitchen opened.

It was too soon for her mother and son to be back from walking the dog. Ezzie lifted her gaze from the bowl and smiled. "Nate!"

"Ezzie! Hey!" he said as he walked through the door.

Leaving the spoon in the bowl, she jogged around the kitchen island, wrapped her arms around her brother's shoulders and hugged him tightly. She had never been so happy—

Luke stepped into the kitchen and stopped just inside the door.

Oh shit. This was not happening. Her ex-boyfriend, her son's father, had not just waltz into her parents' house.

She blinked.

Nothing changed. Luke still stood in the doorway, his chocolate-brown eyes staring blankly at her. All six foot of him was dressed in a pair of khakis and a light-blue polo shirt.

She swallowed. Not good.

Nate released the hug. "What are you doing here? I didn't think you were coming."

Focus. You have to focus. Look away, that's exactly what she had to do. Plastering a fake grin on her face, Ezzie turned her attention back to her brother. "Um, yeah. I had a last-minute change of plans."

"Does that mean Joey's here too?"

"Yes, but he's out with—"

A little, white fluff-ball bounded into the kitchen and began yapping at their feet. She hadn't heard the front door open, but the return of her mother's Maltese only indicated one thing. Her world was about to get flipped upside down for the second time in less than five minutes.

"Lola!" Joey ran into the kitchen after the dog. Her son screeched to a halt. "Uncle Nate!"

"Hey, kiddo." Nate scooped Joey up and gave him a hard squeeze.

Ezzie shifted her eyes from the reunion between her son and brother to Luke.

His eyes widened and flitted from Joey back to her, then back again.

She didn't have to keep looking to know what was going through his head. This was a moment she had half-prepared for over the last few years. God, she hoped he kept his cool.

With Joey in his arms, Nate turned around. "Hey, I want you to meet someone. This is my good friend, Luke. Luke, this is my nephew Joey."

Luke swallowed. He was not seeing this. A set of brown eyes much like his own peered back at him. There was no way in hell this little boy was his son.

No way in hell Ezzie would keep something like this from him.

He had to be imagining things.

The continuous yapping of the tiny dog snapped him out of la-la land and brought him back to the present.

Ezzie picked up the dog and handed the tiny thing to her mother. When had Mrs. Donovan come into the kitchen? He hadn't even noticed her. All he could see was the little boy, who looked—wait, Nate had said something.

Yeah, dumbass. He introduced the kid. Right, an introduction. He needed to say something.

"Uh, hi."

"Hi," Joey said.

The little boy turned back to Nate. "Does this make him my uncle too?"

Nate chuckled. "No, but I'm sure Luke wouldn't mind if you called him that."

"Uncle Luke. I like that."

Luke studied Joey. The two of them didn't just share eye color. Joey's dark brown hair—the same as his. Those little fingers—the same as his. He ran a hand through his hair. God, he really had to be imagining all this. Quietly inhaling a deep breath, he cast his gaze at Ezzie.

No matter what he was thinking, the answer laid with her.

Rubbing her hands, Ezzie glanced from him to her son. "Joey, why don't you go wash your hands? Then you can help me finish these cupcakes."

There was a slight panic in those sapphire blue eyes of hers. One she obviously failed to conceal, at least from him. It confirmed all the thoughts running through his head.

She had hidden his son from him for five years.

Five fucking years!

"Yes, Mommy." Joey wiggled free from Nate's hold and ran down the hallway.

"No running!" Ezzie called out. "And make sure you use soap."

"Don't worry, sis. I'll make sure he does it right," Nate said.

Good. If Nate went off for a few minutes to help Joey wash his hands, he could have that time to talk to Ezzie. She had a lot of explaining to do. Sure, he believed with everything he saw with his own eyes that her son was his son. But confirmation would go a long way. Luke strode over to the counter by the kitchen sink and leaned against it.

"Thanks. Um, hey." She grabbed Nate's arm. "I have something I need to talk to you about later."

"You going to be here all weekend?"

"That's the plan."

Did she glimpse at him? Had she really just looked at him out of her periphery? Like his presence had put a kink in her plan. Luke crossed his arms. He had no intention of throwing a wrench in whatever she had going on, but he sure as hell would do what was necessary to get to the truth.

He had that right.

Fuck. This was not going well. Not at all. Ezzie chewed on the inside of her cheek as she peered back at her brother. She didn't want him to see how nervous she was, but she had to stress the importance of what she had to talk to him about. Then again, it probably had more to do with the fact that Luke kept glaring at her as if she had stolen something from him.

In a sense, she had, but she couldn't address that right then. She focused entirely on her brother. "We have to talk about it tonight."

"All right. We can do that. Now, I'm going to go check on my nephew." Nate disappeared down the hallway.

Without her brother as a buffer, she did the only thing she could. She picked the spoon back up and returned to stirring the mix. If she kept her attention on that for the next few minutes, she could avoid the inevitable. *Don't look,* she told herself. *Just don't look.* Her eyes lifted from the bowl to Luke of their own volition. *Damn it!*

Luke narrowed his eyes at her. "Care to explain what the hell just happened?"

All she had to do was not look, but no, she couldn't do that. He had a white-knuckled grip on the counter. Despite the obvious anger in his stature, he still looked as handsome as the first day they met. His broad shoulders, bulging biceps, strong jaw-line, and deep-set, chocolate-brown eyes still called out to her. None of that changed their situation.

Dropping her gaze back to the bowl, Ezzie scraped the sides and stirred the mixture some more. "What are you talking about? I mean, you met my son, but I thought that was pretty obvious."

"Don't play dumb, Ezzie. It doesn't suit you."

"Excuse me?" Her head snapped up. She swallowed.

Luke pushed off the counter and inched closer to the kitchen island. His nostrils flared and he jabbed a finger in her face. "He looks like me. Same eyes, same hair, same hands and don't even try to tell me I'm seeing things."

She could handle this one of two ways. Deny the blatant truth, though there wasn't much evidence to support the denial. Even Luke's mother had mentioned on a few occasions over the years how much Joey looked like him. Or, she could get it over with and admit what stared him in the face not a minute ago.

She set the spoon aside. Ezzie leaned on the counter of the kitchen island. "What if he does? Joey and I have done perfectly fine without your help."

His eyes widened, and then narrowed. With a vein in his neck bulging, Luke cracked his neck. "Fine? You've done fine? Why the hell didn't you tell me you were pregnant?"

Oh, he had a lot of nerve. Like she hadn't tried. More than once too. Not just when she'd first found out either. How many unanswered letters had she sent? And that phone call? His graduation—she couldn't really count that. She hadn't stayed long.

Ezzie grinded her jaw. "I did try to tell you."

"When? Because I'm fairly certain I'd remember a conversation where you told me you were pregnant."

Ezzie crossed her arms. This was getting them nowhere. Truthfully, she could explain everything, but like he'd recall the day he broke her heart and shut her out of his life. "You do not get to guilt trip me. I wasn't going to be an obligation back then, my son and I sure as hell won't be now."

"You have never—"

Joey bolted back into the kitchen and skidded to a stop in front of Ezzie. "All washed, Mommy."

She had a small idea as to the direction Luke's statement had been about to take, but she was grateful it hadn't. He was the least of her concerns right now.

Uncrossing her arms, she turned toward her son. "Both sides?"

"'Course I did."

"Let me see."

Her son held out his hands. Crouching down on her haunches, she took each of his hands in her own and inspected them. It wasn't necessary, but she always did it. It had become a game between them. One time she even broke out white gloves to check for dirt. He had giggled for a good five minutes back then. God, she remembered that like it was yesterday.

"I pass 'spection, Mommy?"

"Yes, you have." Beaming brightly, Ezzie kissed her son's cheek and tickled his stomach.

Joey laughed. "Mommy, stop!"

"All right." She rose to her full height and ruffled the top of her son's head. Her brother moseyed into the kitchen. Perfect timing. "Why don't you go with Uncle Nate and get a chair so we can finish these cupcakes?"

"I got it," Luke said.

Before she had a chance to object, he'd dashed around the kitchen island and started for the dining room.

Nate folded his arms across his chest and eyeballed Ezzie. "What is it you wanted to talk to me about?"

"Later. Now isn't the time." Never mind the whole legal thing. That was bad enough. If her arrest was the freaking cake, then Luke's presence was the icing. She'd never planned for her brother to find out about that. God, she hoped he didn't. He'd never forgive her for lying to him about Joey's father.

"If that's what you want."

"Yep."

That was exactly what she wanted. And with her son in the other room getting a chair with his biological father, she intended to focus more on that than her arrest. Biting the inside of her bottom lip, Ezzie glanced toward the dining room. What the hell was taking them so long?

"You okay, sis? You look like your favorite vendor just went out of business. You're not in trouble or anything, are you?"

Her brother would notice her internal emotional rollercoaster right then, wouldn't he? "You could say that. I promise, I'll explain it all later."

"I'm going to hold you to that."

"We got the chair, Mommy." Joey and Luke returned each carrying one side of a wooden chair.

Digging his elbow into his knee, Luke massaged the back of his neck. How the hell could Ezzie not have told him about his son? And what the hell did she mean by she tried to tell him? What load of crap was she trying to sell? She hadn't called him. She hadn't written him. She hadn't shown up on his doorstep. She hadn't done anything. Damn it. He seriously needed to talk to her. There were so many things they had to figure out.

Now that he knew about his son, he certainly planned to be a part of his life. Therein laid the problem. How was he supposed to be involved when his son lived in California and he lived here in Utah? He couldn't just uproot himself; he'd have to leave his law firm behind. And how in the hell would he explain that to Nate?

Inwardly sighing, Luke leaned back on the couch and glanced at Nate. Yeah, how exactly was he supposed to explain he'd knocked up his sister?

Shit, he thought. Maybe he should figure all this out before he pulled Ezzie aside. It wasn't like she was going anywhere. At least not for the weekend.

This was just like in court. He came up with a plan and executed it. It was the most reasonable solution. Nodding to himself, Luke stood. "I'm going to head back home."

"Sure, man. I'll see you in the morning."

Luke frowned. The words had come out of Nate's mouth, but there hadn't been much conviction in them. He didn't even look up, all of which was completely out of character.

"You okay?"

"I don't know." Nate steepled his fingers. "Ezzie said she had to talk to me about something. Some kind of trouble, but she hasn't elaborated or given me a whole lot of information. I'm waiting for her to finish putting Joey to bed so we can talk."

Trouble? Trouble wasn't anything he wanted to hear. What he wanted right then was to clear his head and figure things out, not to have to deal with another problem, but what if it was serious? What if she required some serious legal help? He'd never forgive himself if he just up and left. Shit.

Luke dragged a hand down his face. "I'll—"

"Okay. I finally got him to sleep. We can..." Ezzie's gaze paused on him. She swallowed and turned to Nate. "Why don't we go talk in the kitchen?"

"What's wrong with where we're at?"

"Nothing, I guess," she said.

Luke crossed his arms. He was the problem. He wouldn't imagine she'd come out and say it because then it would be admitting the truth to Nate. Hmm, he could offer to give them some privacy, but he was damn curious as to what was going on.

Nate cocked an eyebrow and gestured to him. "You do know Luke is my business partner, right? So, whatever you have to say stays between the three of us."

Ezzie eyeballed both of them. "You swear? Swear that what I'm about to tell you Mom and Dad do not find out about. Swear to it."

Standing, Nate narrowed his eyes. "What the hell is going on? Why do I have to swear not to tell Mom and Dad?"

"Because I don't want Joey finding out. Now swear."

"Fine, I swear," Nate said.

God, this had to be bad. Really bad. The last time he remembered her family not knowing about something had been when she told him about her tattoo. The memory of their weekend camping crept into his brain. Luke shook it away. *Not now.*

Whatever was going on warranted her talking. Now. Too bad he wasn't any more prepared for what she said next than when he saw his son run into the kitchen. "I swear, too."

She inhaled and exhaled deeply. "I got arrested two days ago."

"What?!" Luke practically shouted.

"Shh, keep your voice down." Crikey. She expected her brother to holler at her more than she did Luke.

Instead, Nate stood there in silence staring at her with wide eyes. After a second, he rubbed the top of his brow with his thumb. "I'm sorry; did you say you got arrested? For what?"

"Embezzlement and a whole slew of other charges." She couldn't list all of them, but they all apparently linked back to that first one. This is why she had the defense attorney she'd met with back home write it all down for her. She dug out a sheet of paper and held it out to her brother. "Here; this is everything I'm being charged with."

Nate snagged the sheet of paper and paced from one end of the couch to the other. "Seriously, Ezzie? Embezzlement, security fraud, Ponzi-like scheme, money laundering, and interstate transportation of stolen property. How the hell did this happen?"

"I don't know. The lawyer back home kept saying something about investors in my bakery, but I haven't had any in three years." All she knew was that the charges weren't magically going to go away. Nothing else about them made any sense. She'd called her accountant before getting on her flight there to try and figure it out, but Jonathan hadn't answered.

"This is why I need your help. I need you to represent me."

"I'm sorry, but I can't do that."

"What? Why?" There wouldn't be any sort of conflict. She'd do everything he told her to do, even if she hated the idea. And it wasn't like he'd be representing someone guilty. It wasn't a complicated situation.

"At least two of these are felony charges. I handle misdemeanors. I wouldn't take the chance in screwing your case up due to incompetency on my end."

"But I trust you." That was settled. Her brother would represent her and life would move forward. They just had to keep it all a secret from her parents and son.

"I wouldn't even know where to begin."

Ezzie didn't either, but she had faith he'd figure it out. "I believe—"

"I'll do it," Luke said.

"Excuse me?" She didn't just hear that. Nope, no way Luke had volunteered to represent her. She must have hallucinated the whole thing. But why would she do that? Yeah, he was still as handsome as ever. It didn't matter that she'd been fighting the butterflies all evening. He was her ex for a reason, which was exactly why she had misheard him.

"I'll take on your case. I'll represent you." Luke uncrossed his arms and held his hand out for the sheet of paper she'd given Nate.

Nate handed Luke the paper. "Thanks, man. You're better equipped to handle this."

Ezzie glanced from Nate to Luke. This had insanity written all over it. Not only would they be forced to spend time together, but they'd have to have the inevitable conversation about Joey. She narrowed her eyes. That was the point, wasn't it? It would give him the opportunity to be around her son. Oh no, this would not do. She opened her mouth and snapped it shut.

Shit. If she objected, her brother would want to know why. And she wouldn't be able to answer that. Not without revealing her and Luke's history. She was stuck. Great, just fucking great.

"What do we do first?"

"You don't do anything. As for me, I'll work on getting a pro hac vice motion going, which will allow me to represent you. I'll also get my secretary to pull California state laws." Luke paused for a moment. With a little sparkle in his eyes, he stroked his chin. "Actually, I do need something from you."

"What's that?" What could he possibly need? After all that, he sounded like he had taken the reigns and gotten the horse moving.

"Your flight information, so I can make sure we're all heading out together."

"Right."

Ezzie frowned. Of course, he planned for them to fly back to California together. Why didn't she think of that?

Two

LUKE GRINNED. THERE'D BE NO hiding from him now. Ezzie would have to answer his questions and give him the chance to get to know his son. He slapped his hands together. "Looks like I've got some work to do, so I'll bid you both a good night."

"Thanks again, man." Nate and Luke clasped hands and shook.

He nodded and headed for the kitchen. He really shouldn't be this happy given the circumstances. The charges Ezzie was facing weren't minor. It really was going to be a lot of work, possibly long nights, but that was only part of what he loved about being a lawyer. The other part was seeing justice prevail.

Placing his hand on the doorknob, he stopped. The legal stuff would be easier than the rest of it. Working with her, spending time with her, and getting to know his son in the mix ... was he truly ready for all that?

"Luke, wait," Ezzie called out. She paused a few feet away from him. "Why are you doing this?"

Peering over his shoulder, he took his hand off the doorknob and turned around. His eyebrows furrowed. It was a pretty open-ended question. Was she referring to him leaving or choosing to represent her?

"Doing what?"

"Taking on my case. Why are you doing it? To help Nate? To help me? Or is it because of Joey?"

There were a lot of reasons he had opted to help. Nate was one. He didn't like the idea of his best friend appearing helpless. Then there was the added benefit of getting to know his son. Though if he were truly honest with himself—

Fuck me, he thought.

Ezzie stood there waiting for his answer in her way too tight, skinny jeans. A sleeveless white blouse. Her long, mahogany hair pulled back in a simple ponytail. His gaze lingered as he took it all in.

He couldn't go there. He had to focus on the secret she'd kept from him all this time, and then he could give her something without owning up to his attraction. *Fuck.* Luke glimpsed past her for a moment, refocused himself and returned his attention to her.

Luke lowered his voice. "If you're asking if I plan to get to know my son, the answer is yes."

"You want to take advantage of the situation, fine. But you need to understand something. He's *my* son. You are nothing but a friend of the family and that is all he needs to know. Got it?"

"You can't seriously expect me not to tell him who I am. He's my son and he deserves to know who his father is." Luke pointed in the direction of the hallway.

She had to have her head up her ass, if she believed for one second he'd stay silent about his relationship to Joey. Would it be something he'd go and blurt out? No. He'd spend time with his son before sharing that vital piece of information. Obviously, it was something that had to be handled delicately. He didn't know what Joey knew about him, but that didn't mean it had to stay quiet any longer.

"I think you've kept it a secret for long enough. Don't you?"

"I—"

"Hey. Everything okay?" Nate waltzed into the kitchen.

Luke nodded. "Yeah. It's fine. Ezzie and I were just talking about the flight to Los Angeles. We might end up leaving tomorrow night after the party instead of Sunday."

The words had flown out of his mouth before he'd even had a chance to register what he was saying, though it made sense to leave sooner rather than later. Not only would it give him more time with Joey, it would give him more prep time for her case. Especially since he'd have to figure out a defense strategy, even if his motion for representation wouldn't be heard before Monday or Tuesday.

"Oh yeah? I hate to see you leave early sis, but I can understand why. There's a lot to do before your next court date," Nate said.

"I'm sure there is. I think I'll head to bed. Good night, Luke." With a smirk, she left the kitchen and disappeared down the hallway.

Nate glimpsed from Ezzie to Luke. "You sure everything is okay?"

"I'm positive. I'll see you tomorrow."

Standing in a small group of Ezzie's parents' friends, Luke scanned the backyard for his son. *His* son. The sound of it was so strange. It had been less than twenty-four hours. No way could he grow accustomed to the term that fast.

How could Ezzie hide this from him? She should've found a way to tell him. Not make up some story about a one-night stand. At least, that's what he heard Nate ramble on and on about. That had been enough to deter him from looking at any pictures.

Now he had to figure out how to get to know his son. No better time than the present. Luke wiped the sweat on his palm down the front of his jeans and surveyed the backyard one more time.

There weren't a whole lot of kids running around. Of the few that had accompanied their parents, most were older ... at least ten or more. Joey was the only four-year-old there.

Probably why his son sat on one of the benches under the large oak tree that had been in the Donovan's backyard for as long as he could remember. It offered a nice shady spot where the kid could—had the kid actually taken out a book?

"Excuse me." Luke nodded to the group he'd been hanging around and strode across the yard. He gestured to the empty seat on the bench. "Care if I sit here?"

Joey looked up from the book in his hands. "Nope."

Luke sat next to his son. Ezzie would kill him if she saw where he was, but she had disappeared. Besides, he wasn't going to say or do anything stupid. "What are you reading?"

"Superman."

"Oh? Is he your favorite superhero?" He examined the book his son held. It wasn't a typical comic book, but an actual book just with bigger pictures and fewer words. He'd never seen anything like that before.

"After my daddy."

What did he say? Did he say his father? Luke blinked. He truly figured if he didn't know about his son that his son didn't know about him. He knew he couldn't outright ask if Joey knew who he was. No. Unless … he did it discreetly.

He swallowed. "Is your dad … is he a, uh, superhero?"

"Yes. Mommy tells me stories about his rescues all the time."

Rescues? Wait—Ezzie told him stories? He glanced toward the house. She talked about him? How was he supposed to be upset with her if she actually made sure their son knew of him? God, he had no idea what to think about all this.

"Uncle Luke, I'm hungry. Can you make me a hot dog?"

His shoulders tensed at the term *uncle*. He despised that word. It was an awful, torturous word. He'd correct this … as soon as he figured out how. Turning back to his son, Luke nodded. "Yeah. I can do that. What do you want on it? Mayo, mustard, ketchup?"

"Mustard, please."

"Anything else? Relish, maybe?"

Joey screwed up his face. "Yuck!"

"I know how you feel, kid. Your mom is the only one I know who puts that nasty stuff on her hotdog. That and mayo." Luke smirked. He didn't like the chopped-up pickles on his hotdog either. Good to know his son's tastes took after his own. Getting to his feet, he gestured to the picnic table full of food. "Come on, let's get some grub."

Joey giggled and stood. "That's a funny word."

"Yeah, it is." The two of them walked next to each other toward the food table. "So, what's your favorite thing about Superman?"

"He flies!"

"Lucy, just tell everyone we'll meet for an hour Monday morning. I'll explain everything then."

She couldn't meet her employees at the bakery. The government had closed her bakery, citing it as part of the charges she faced. Maybe they could meet at her secondary office. Either that or someplace neutral, but she didn't want everyone knowing her business. And she'd have to explain what was going on to her employees.

Shit. She should probably talk to Luke about it. She still had no idea how he'd wound up being her attorney. That wasn't completely true. She understood the mechanics' it just seemed to have come out of left field. Her brother was supposed to be the one representing her, not her ex-boyfriend.

"I will. Any thoughts on when the bakery might reopen?"

Given what the internet told her, it all depended on whether or not she could prove her innocence. If she was found guilty, she'd go away for a long time. She'd never see her son grow up and the bakery would shut down for good. All the hard work she'd put in would be gone. But she couldn't tell Lucy that.

"I'm not sure, but I'll address that at the meeting too. Hey, have you heard from Jonathan?"

"Nope. Nothing. Nada."

"A simple no would've sufficed."

Where the hell had her accountant disappeared to? She really needed him to figure out where all this misinformation about her business had been obtained from.

"Should I keep trying him?"

"No, that's okay. I'll plan a trip to his office when I get back."

Pushing off the kitchen island she'd been leaning on, she eyeballed the time on her silver watch. Had she really been away from the party for ten minutes already? Brushing the skirting of her turquoise dress down, she meandered out of the house and into the backyard.

She hadn't gotten more than ten feet when she spotted Luke talking to her son. Oh, hell no. He was not going to do this now. "Hey, Lucy, I gotta go."

Without waiting for a goodbye, Ezzie disconnected the call on her cell phone and strode quickly in their direction. Plastering a smile to her face, she closed in on them. "Joey, honey, why don't you go see what Uncle Nate is doing?"

"But Mommy, I'm talking to Uncle Luke."

"Go, now," Ezzie stated firmly, a tone that every mother learned to utilize when required. She hated having to use it, but she'd be damned if her son discovered something he didn't need to know.

"Yes, ma'am." Joey waved goodbye to Luke and shuffled to the other side of the yard.

"Was that necessary?" Luke scoffed. He hadn't been doing anything wrong. All he'd done was have a conversation with his son.

"Yes. I can't have you going off and telling Joey the truth without knowing you're fully aware of the repercussions."

Frowning, he crossed his arms. Did she think he was stupid? He was well aware of the consequences of his son finding out about him. Although his son knew something, it wasn't everything. He had no intention of outright telling Joey the truth without having some kind of plan in place. "Contrary to popular belief, I'm not an idiot."

"Are you sure about that? Because I'm fairly certain I explicitly said that if you wanted to talk to him, I had to be around. Or did you forget all about that?"

Luke grinded his jaw and advanced a few steps forward. Minimizing the gap between them, he jabbed a finger in her face. "No more than you forgetting to tell me that I had a son."

"I tried to tell you on multiple occasions. But you were too damn busy with your hoity-toity friends or whatever bimbo you were working on for the week."

"Oh, that's bullshit and you know it."

He hadn't been with another woman since she'd come into his life. Even after she left, he couldn't find it in himself to date anyone else. It didn't stop or prevent women from flirting with him; he just wasn't interested.

No one could ever compare.

It was still true. Staring at her in that turquoise and sunflower loose-fitting spring dress that hugged her hourglass figure, he was partially reminded of what attracted him in the first place. It wasn't just her looks, but the warmth he often felt whenever they were together. Despite his anger with her, his body hummed being this close to her. Not that he would reveal any of that.

Ezzie popped out a hip and narrowed her eyes. "Which part? Your stuck-up friends? Or that you collect women?"

"While neither is true, I was referring to you telling me about our son. I sure as hell would've remembered that." Because if he had found out about Joey any time in the last five years, he would've manned up. Yeah, Harvard had been a great school, but any law school could've given him the same education. The school didn't make him a lawyer; it simply provided him the necessary tools.

"Really? You positive about that? Because I seem to recall you kissing some blonde the first time I tried to tell you. Then there was the woman who answered your phone the second time. That was just in the beginning." She scoffed.

He blinked. The day she saw his ex-girlfriend kiss him was the first time? How had he not put two and two together? How had he managed to overlook the timing of her pregnancy? Simple. Nate believed what she'd told him and he believed Nate.

But it wasn't just that. It had also been the guilt over what happened between them and how things had ended. His guilt compiled with what she'd told Nate convinced him he hadn't received something as wonderful as a child with her. It was one of things he had longed to have for their future before it had all been destroyed.

Luke groaned. "I didn't kiss her and I would've told you that if you hadn't run off."

"You think that would've been enough to assure me that I wasn't just another rung in the ladder?"

Oh, you were definitely not just another woman, he thought. Ezzie had been—

No. He refused to go there. He refused to be sucked in by those bright blue eyes, those long, silky brown locks, those pouty lips, or that curvaceous body of hers. That was not a direction they needed to go. Luke gripped the back of his neck and sighed heavily. He could admit one thing.

"You were not another notch in my bed post. I—"

The punch came out of nowhere. One second Luke was standing there prepared to admit something he shouldn't, and the next he was stumbling backwards.

"Nate!" Ezzie exclaimed.

Where the hell had he come from? She hadn't even seen him until his knuckles connected with Luke's jaw.

"What the fuck were you thinking? She's my little sister!" Nate yelled.

Oh, this was not good. Not good at all. Her brother was never supposed to find out; then again, her pregnancy with Joey kind of made it inevitable. Instead, it was just a matter of time. Either way, this was neither the place nor the time for this to occur.

"Nate—"

Luke wiped the blood from the corner of his lip and proceeded to close the distance between them. "I was thinking she's a grown-ass woman who didn't need her brother choosing guys for her. Did you ever bother to tell her your plan? Or were you too much of a coward to ever admit the truth?"

Growling, Nate charged at Luke.

With a small sidestep, he dodged Nate's attempt to grapple him. Using the momentum of the lunge, Luke hooked an arm around Nate's neck and kneed him in the gut.

"Stop it!" Ezzie yelled.

Forget about asking her brother what Luke meant. She had to get them to quit fighting. But they were too close together for her to get in the middle.

Not backing down, Nate balled up his fist and punched Luke in the side over and over until he released his hold. With his windpipe no longer being crushed, Nate thrust his shoulder into Luke's chest and knocked him to the ground.

Seeing her only chance to intervene, Ezzie jumped between Nate and Luke before her brother advanced on Luke again. "Stop it!"

"Get out of the way, Ezzie!"

"Absolutely not. Not unless you can be civil."

She didn't think it was too much to ask. Yeah, her brother overheard something she didn't mean for him to ever discover. Nothing she could do about it now, aside from preventing him and her ex-boyfriend from continuing to beat the shit out of one another.

"You're my little sister. He knew you were off limits."

"Excuse me? Last I checked, I'm an adult and—"

It wasn't Luke getting to his feet that interrupted her statement. It was the short flash of dark brown hair that she caught out of the corner of her eye that made her stop. She turned around in time to witness the first of many offenses to come from her son.

"You leave my Uncle Nate alone!" Joey kicked Luke in the shin and then took off toward the house.

"Joseph!"

Her son didn't stop when she hollered his name. Great, just great. Now she was going to have to punish her son for mimicking the stupid example set by her brother and ex-boyfriend.

Ezzie glared at the two of them. "I hope you're both happy."

No sooner had those words left her mouth had her mother stormed over in their direction. Icing on the fucking cake. For five seconds she'd forgotten her brother and ex-boyfriend had been fighting in the backyard of her parents' house, where multiple people had come out to celebrate her parents' anniversary.

"Lucas Daniel Jonnihan and Nathan Marcus Donovan, what the hell is wrong with you?" her mother hollered.

"He started it," Luke and Nate uttered and pointed at each other simultaneously.

"I don't care. It ends, right now. Do you both understand me?"

"Yes ma'am," they both said again at the same time.

Ezzie bit the inside of her cheek. They may have both agreed, but she could see by the fire in each of their eyes that the agreement wouldn't last. Whatever. Either way, she had to get her son away from this. She had more than enough to deal with back home. "I'm sorry, Mom, but I think Joey and I should head back to California tonight."

"What? You've hardly been here a day."

"I know. I'm really sorry. We'll come out and say goodbye before we leave." She gave her mother a quick hug and headed into the house.

"I don't know what in the world the two of you were fighting over, but you need to fix it. Apologize. Now," Mrs. Donovan hissed.

Shit. Luke eyeballed Ezzie and Nate's mother. Apologizing to Nate would be the right thing, but he didn't throw the first punch so he refused to apologize first. But he did need to excuse himself so he could convince Ezzie to stay one more night. Tomorrow would come soon enough, and once they got to California, they had to hit the ground running. Her next court appearance was a little over a week away and there was a lot they had to cover, but none of it was anything he could admit to Ezzie's mother.

He promised not to say anything and he planned to keep it that way. However, if he worded his statement carefully, he could slip away without apologizing. "You're right, Mrs. Donovan. We were both acting like Neanderthals. Please forgive my behavior. Let me make it up to you by getting Ezzie to stay the night."

"Do you think you can? This is the most I've seen them in six months. It's so hard with them being so far away."

Six months? He knew Ezzie's family visited her in California. From the way Nate acted, he didn't know Joey was his son, but what about her parents? Did they know? No. No way. They'd never been told about his relationship with Ezzie. Or so he presumed.

Luke squeezed Ezzie's mother's shoulder. "Of course."

"That would mean the world to me. Thank you."

With a quick nod, he turned around and proceeded toward the house. Now, how would he persuade Ezzie to leave tomorrow instead? He didn't have a whole lot of options. Then again, there was that one, but that would mean he'd have to blackmail her and that wouldn't be a great start to their attorney/client relationship.

Shit. There had to be a better choice than threatening to tell her parents she'd been arrested.

"Joseph Lucas, do not argue with me," Ezzie snapped.

She snagged her suitcase and her son's backpack out of the closet of her old bedroom.

Her parents had redecorated it after she'd moved out. It no longer looked like her bedroom. Her posters had been replaced with two paintings, one above the bed and the other on the opposite wall, both landscape portraits. Nothing that really stood out. She sighed, eyeing the bed that had once belonged to her. Even the bed appeared plain and boring.

What had she been thinking coming home this weekend? With her son, nonetheless. Why hadn't she taken Matt up on his offer to watch Joey? Because she hadn't expected Luke to be there. Ezzie handed her son his backpack.

Joey knocked the bag out of her hands. "I don't wanna go home."

"It isn't your decision. Now pick the backpack up, go to the living room, and get your toys. Right this instance." She grinded her jaw. She had spanked her son once in the four years and three months since his birth. Most of his attitude she suspected came from her, though it was possible he got some from Luke too. One of the many things she often wondered about.

"But, Mommy—"

"No buts. Go." She pointed at the bedroom door.

He didn't utter another word. Joey grabbed his backpack off the floor, hung his head, and shuffled into the hallway.

None of this was supposed to be difficult. It was supposed to be a simple trip. Her son would get to enjoy time with his grandparents and she could see her brother all while convincing him to fly out to California to be her attorney. Simple? Right. Simple.

A knock on the bedroom door caused her to jerk back. Her eyes flitted to the doorway. "Jesus! What the hell is wrong with you?"

Luke held his hands up in defense. "Sorry. I wasn't trying to scare you."

"What do you want?" She bit the inside of her cheek. She could see a bruise blossoming on his lower jaw. Probably meant he had bruises forming on his outer ribcage too. Forcing herself to look away, Ezzie turned toward the closet and removed a couple of dresses she'd hung up yesterday afternoon.

"To apologize. I shouldn't have argued with you over Joey and I shouldn't have egged your brother on in the fight. I know I didn't help anything."

Laying the dresses across the bed, she glanced over her shoulder. She hadn't expected that. The apology or the clear-cut reason for it. Something he'd never done in the past. "Then why did you?"

"Because I'm in shock, Ez. I'm not exactly sure how to handle this. Obviously, I've dealt with this poorly. But I promise we'll figure it out. Please, just don't take it out on your parents. Today is about them."

He had no clue if what he said worked. Ezzie just stared at him and he couldn't blame her. But he'd done the only thing he could. He spoke from the heart. God, he couldn't recall the last time he'd done that. No, that's not true. It had been the day he walked away from her door. Not one of his best memories. And certainly not one he wanted to think about right then either. He was trying to be positive.

Luke held his hand out. "Shall we get back to the party?"

Joey slipped in past him and stopped between him and Ezzie. "I'm ready to go, Mommy."

"It's okay. We're going to stay one more night."

"Yay!" Joey dropped his backpack and jumped up and down.

Ezzie laced her fingers together in front of her belly and turned her attention to their son. "Before we do, you owe Mr. Luke an apology."

"I do?"

"Yes, you do. We don't kick other people. Defending someone else or not, fighting resolves nothing." She shifted her gaze toward Luke.

Ouch. Her words stung, but he got the picture. As much as he hated the idea, he should probably apologize to Nate when they got back outside, if his best friend was even still around or would accept it. He really hadn't been thinking by dragging Ezzie into a conversation they had to have about their son. God, that was so strange. *Their* son.

"I'm sorry, Mr. Luke. I shouldn't have kicked you." Joey looked from Luke back to his mother. "Can I go back outside now?"

"Yes, you may, but no running. We'll be right behind you."

"Thanks, Mommy." Joey hustled out of the bedroom door and down the hallway.

It would take him some time to get accustomed to this little boy being his son, let alone *their* son. Even with everything going on, she still tried to teach right from wrong. Luke sighed and gripped the back of his neck. "Is this your way of telling me I should apologize to your brother?"

"Technically, you both should apologize to each other, but I don't suspect he'll listen at the moment. Give him some time to calm down."

"Think he'll ever forgive me?"

The question popped out before he could stop it. They had talked about this once before. It was the reason she had run out of the hotel room that night. God, he had to stop thinking about the past. It was in the past.

"Never mind, don't answer that. Let's just get back to the party. We can leave for California in the morning as planned."

Ezzie started toward him and paused. "You're still going to represent me?"

"Of course."

"Why?"

The answer was simple and complicated at the same time. Aside from his desire to get to know his son and figure out some kind of arrangement with her, she needed him and somewhere deep down, he needed her. Not that he intended to admit that. Ever. Go with the acceptable. Yeah, the acceptable.

"Because you need a good defense attorney."

There was something he wasn't saying, but she wouldn't push the issue. It was going to be difficult enough with her case and him. The fewer obstacles they had to deal with, the easier the next few weeks or so would go.

Ezzie nodded. "Okay."

"Okay."

They headed down the hallway side-by-side toward the back doors. She placed her hand on the handle of the French door and halted. Rejoining the party was a necessity, but there was something she had to do beforehand.

She peered back at Luke. "Thank you."

"For what?"

"For taking my case. I know there's a lot of work ahead of us and I can't imagine any of this is easy, but I appreciate it. I can't tell you what it means to me."

All she'd been able to think about since her arrest had been her son. What would happen to him if she wound up in jail for the next some-odd years? Who would take care of him? Would he even be able to understand what was going on? He was a little over four. He was smart for his age, but even this was beyond his comprehension. Most days it was beyond her comprehension.

Luke hesitantly reached out, then dropped his hand. "Ez, I'd do pretty much anything for you."

"Still, thank you."

She stared at him a moment. It had been the second time he had attempted contact with her. It was likely nothing. Just an unintentional move. Yet ... no. He had hurt her a long time ago. And that was all she had to remember.

Without any further hesitation, she walked out to the backyard.

Three

EZZIE UNLOCKED THE DOOR TO her apartment. About a year after Joey was born, she got her own place. Although she stayed in the same complex, she and Matt agreed separate apartments were for the best. The new place made a great difference and gave her son his own space, where the majority of his toys remained when they weren't scattered across the living room floor. Thankfully, her best friend opted to house-sit while they were gone.

She opened the door. "Matt, we're home."

Joey rushed inside the apartment. He slid the strap of his backpack from his shoulder and dropped it on the floor next to the couch.

"Absolutely not. That doesn't go there. Take that to your bedroom."

"But Mommy, I have to go potty," Joey said.

"Then go the bathroom and come back for it, but it doesn't stay there. Do you understand me?" She pulled her suitcase inside the door and shut it behind her. If her son had his way, he'd leave his stuff wherever it landed. She had no clue where he picked that habit up from. She kept her things put away where they belonged.

"Yes ma'am." He spun around and hustled down the hallway to the bathroom. The door closed two seconds later.

Matt strolled out of her bedroom from the back-right corner. Joey had been given the bedroom directly in front. She hated that his bedroom was first, but the neighborhood was safe and they had a doorman.

"Is it just me, or did you get hit by a tornado while you were away?" He gestured to her appearance.

She regarded herself. Her hair was perfectly straight. These were her best skinny jeans. She'd been thrilled when she hadn't needed to suck in her gut to get them on. And the t-shirt was comfortable and sarcastic. Though maybe referring to whiskey being worth a shot wasn't the most mom thing in her closet, it had been a long flight. That was more about the company than anything else. Her Chucks completed the outfit, plus they were comfortable.

Ezzie lifted her gaze back to him. "What's wrong with what I have on?"

"Nothing. I just didn't expect you to be so put together. That's why I'm wondering if a tornado hit because Dorothy, you are not in Kansas anymore."

Rolling her eyes, she ambled toward her bedroom with the suitcase rolling behind her. Okay. Maybe she had taken a little extra time getting dressed before they'd left. Maybe she had put in a little more effort. Not that she could explain why.

Bullshit, her subconscious screamed at her. *Oh, shut up!* She had spent close to the last forty-eight hours trying not to acknowledge how gorgeous Luke looked. Or how he still turned her stomach into a frigging trampoline. God, this was all a bad idea. A really bad idea.

"Let's just say there were a few bumps in the road."

"Uh oh. I don't like the sound of this."

"Neither do I, but I'm not sure I have much of a choice."

Actually, she didn't have a choice. Her brother may not have spoken to either her or Luke since the day before, but that hadn't altered her faith in his judgment. He'd been adamant that Luke was her best option when it came to a defense attorney. At least that had been his stance prior to him finding out about their ... history.

"How is that even possible?"

She hefted her suitcase onto her bed. Why didn't she text Matt everything last night? Would've saved her the trouble of having to explain it now. "Luke showed up."

"I'm sorry, excuse me. Sandra Dee said what?"

The bathroom door flew open. "Mommy, I'm hungry."

She shook her head. Matt's response didn't shock her any more than her son's request for food. Ezzie shucked her Chucks, put them on the floor of the closet and held up a finger. "Let me get him a snack and I promise I will tell you all."

"I'm holding you to that because I need every detail."

"Yes, I know, spilling is inevitable." Grinning widely, she stepped out of her bedroom and headed for the kitchen.

"Hey Ashlynn, I wanted to make sure you got the motion I left on your desk last night."

Luke hung up the three suits he'd packed. There was plenty of room in the closet so he left space between each. He could break them each down, but it wasn't warranted. They'd stay clean and pressed this way, though he could iron them if necessary.

"I did. I've got it all set to be filed with the court clerk first thing in the morning."

"Excellent. Now where are we on the California law books and Miss Donovan's case file?"

He strode back over to the bed of the hotel that had been booked for the next couple of weeks for him. He might have over planned the stay, but he anticipated that would be the minimum time he'd be there. It wasn't as if Ezzie was guilty and they had to work out a plea. He believed in her innocence.

Yeah, she may have kept a huge secret from him, but she didn't have the capacity to rip someone off. She helped people, whether they just wanted a hand out or a hand up. It was one of the reasons he'd truly fallen for her back then. No matter how he'd seen himself, she only saw the best version of him. She'd seen everything he could be. God, he really had to stop thinking about that.

Luke collected a pile of t-shirts he'd brought for when he could dress down a little and proceeded to the dresser. At least this was a nice hotel.

"The law books should be delivered tomorrow afternoon. As for the case file, the District Attorney's office has assured me it will be sent first thing in the morning."

"Good. I need to dive into this head first. Keep me apprised of when we get on the docket for the pro hac motion."

That he hoped would be sooner rather than later. It didn't sound like the prosecutor's office intended to prolong this, which could be good and bad. It all depended on the evidence they had against Ezzie.

"Yes, sir. Is there anything else I can do?"

"Not at the moment, Ashlynn. Enjoy the rest of your Sunday. I really appreciate you working on your weekend off."

"Not a problem, sir. Have a good day." The line disconnected.

He hung up his cell phone. The next few weeks were going to be interesting to say the least. Luke rubbed his eyes and turned back to his suitcase. After he finished putting his clothes away, he had to come up with a plan of attack for tomorrow. The evidence would really help in knowing the direction they had to take, but there was some information he could collect from Ezzie in the meantime. Anything she could tell him about her bakery would prove helpful in her defense. She'd also have records of her own. Or copies. All of her original records would be in evidence and her bakery would be off limits. Still, that gave him an executable plan.

As long as they could keep their conversation to business.

He sighed. That would prove easier said than done.

On both their parts.

Shit, shit, shit, Matt thought.

None of what Ezzie had spent the last hour telling him was good. Why couldn't this guy have just stayed gone? "Wait a minute. Let me see if I understand this correctly. Your ex-boyfriend not only volunteered to defend you, but did so after finding out about his son?"

"Yes."

"And he's here. In Los Angeles."

Narrowing his eyes, Matt frowned. This outright blew. And not in the fun way. Would Luke remember him? It had been over four years since they'd unintentionally met. Though, if he never showed up at the apartment, then they probably wouldn't cross paths.

Ezzie cocked an eyebrow. "Of course he is. How else is he supposed to defend me?"

"I don't know. By proxy?" He smirked.

"That's not even funny. This is my life on the line we're talking about."

He had to stop. At this rate, she'd see right through him and know something was amiss. The longer he could put off her finding out the truth, the better. Matt clasped her forearm. "I'm sorry, honey. You're right. I know how serious this is. I guess I wasn't expecting to ever see him."

"Yeah. I never thought you guys would meet either. Then again, I didn't plan on him finding out about Joey like this, but it is what it is."

Hell, he never figured the guy would find out period. Not that he thought Ezzie would ever get arrested. Their life had been perfect before that. Now not only was her life at risk, but all the secrets he'd kept from her over the last few years were in jeopardy of coming out.

He studied her. Her blue eyes glazed over, like they did when her mind had gone somewhere sad or dark. Matt grasped her hand in his own. He'd just have to do everything in his power to keep his secrets from being revealed. No matter the cost. "What do you need from me? I'll do whatever I can to help."

"Can you take Joey to school in the morning? Luke is planning to come over here first thing tomorrow to work."

"Here, as in your apartment?" Matt's eyes widened.

Sure, he didn't live here, but he spent more time at Colin's place or her place than he did his own, which only happened to be three doors down. That definitely put a kink in his plan for the past to stay right where it was—in the past. Great. Now what? He scratched his forehead.

"You're okay with that, right?"

Absolutely. I'd love to take a chance in running into your ex-boyfriend and then having to explain how we know each other. Shit.

This is what he got for interfering when he should've left Ezzie to make her own decisions. Wrong or right. Too bad he couldn't go back and change it. He'd just have to do whatever was necessary to avoid running into Luke.

Matt swallowed the lump sitting in his throat. "Sure. Of course I am. No reason not to be. Listen, why I don't I go order pizza for dinner and let you relax a bit."

"That sounds great. Thank you. I really appreciate all your help."

Luke eyed the various buildings as the taxi drove through downtown Los Angeles toward Ezzie's complex. He hated the idea that she was in an apartment and not in a house. His son should have a backyard he could run around and play in. He couldn't really say much though; he lived in an apartment too. There didn't seem to be a reason to rush off and find a house. He spent most of his time at the office anyway.

That would be something he'd have to rectify. Maybe he could search for a house with an office after he got back. He and Ezzie would have to work out some sort of custody arrangement. Then he could work from home whenever he had Joey. The idea had merit. Luke dug his cell phone out of the inside pocket of his jacket and created a reminder; he preferred the backup of ideas and information.

A text came through.

Motion hearing at Clara Shortridge Foltz, 8:30 A.M. tomorrow.

Excellent. A quick response on his motion was a good thing. Luke tucked his phone back in the inside jacket pocket.

The taxi slowed down and pulled alongside the curb. "Here we are, sir."

It hadn't taken much time to get there. He lifted his eyes to the brick building to his right. How long had it been since he'd last been here? He'd only seen Ezzie through a doorway to the living room; not that she'd noticed him. Based on what he'd seen back then he would've guessed she had been about six months pregnant at the time. And his son had turned four a couple of months ago. That made it ... a little over four and half years. The building hadn't changed much.

Luke shifted his gaze to the corner of the tall building. The glass doors appeared to be in the same spot. From what he could tell, the only difference between now and back then—Ezzie's apartment number.

He pulled his wallet out of his pocket, eyeballed the cost for his ride and handed the driver a twenty-dollar bill. "Keep the change."

Surveying the building again, he climbed out of the vehicle and headed toward the entrance. Luke walked through a set of glass doors. An elegant lobby welcomed him the same as it had before. A shiny tan marble floor with an intricate design stared back at him.

Last time he had crossed through this lobby, no one had been at the large desk to his right, nor had anyone occupied the sitting area beside him. The same Oriental rug; no, that might be different. But the vinyl covered chairs and burnt orange couch hadn't changed. It was the same with the glass table atop the patterned rug. It was just as inviting as it had been before.

It was the same with the two large columns that stood between him and another set of glass doors. The doors that separated the rest of the building from the outside world. The doors that give him access to the person he'd come to see. Something else that hadn't changed.

"How can I help you, sir?" a clerk behind the desk questioned, interrupting the memories running through his head.

Shaking the painful thoughts away, he refocused on his reason for being there. "Um, Luke Jonnihan to see Esmeralda Donovan."

The clerk typed something into what he assumed was a computer. He couldn't really tell from this angle.

Ezzie's leg bounced as she patiently waited for the elevator to hit the first floor and let her out. The thing was taking forever today. It didn't normally do this. Most days she swore it took a matter of seconds to get from her seventh-floor apartment to the first floor. Of course, today would be different. The one time she depended on it going quickly and it takes its—

The number one at the top of the elevator lit up. Finally.

The elevator doors slid apart and she exited. Turning to the right, she pushed open a glass door that led into the lobby and stopped. Luke stood at the front desk. He wasn't supposed to be there yet. She wasn't expecting him for another two hours. Isn't that what they agreed on?

"Miss Donovan, I was just about to ring you."

She'd hardly noticed who was behind the desk this morning. At least until his words snapped her out of her reverie. Ezzie blinked and glanced at the desk attendant. "That's okay, James. I've got it from here. Thank you."

She turned her attention to Luke. "You're early."

"Didn't we agree to meet at eight?"

Frowning, she stepped all the way into the lobby and closed the distance between the two of them. He'd probably arrived early in hopes of spending time with her son. Crikey. What would it take for them to get on the same page when it came to Joey?

Whatever. She didn't have time to think about this now. Ezzie grimaced at the time on her watch. Shit. She was running late as it was for her staff meeting. No time to alter plans. He'd just have to come with her. "No, but I guess you can come along."

"Come along? Where are we going?"

"I'm meeting my staff so I can explain to them what's going on. Honestly, it's probably a good thing for you to be there. You might be able to help me answer any questions they might have." Especially as she anticipated there would be plenty she couldn't answer. Like when the bakery would reopen. Or how their wages would be handled. Not only had her business account been frozen, but so had her personal account. She suspected there was only one answer and it all depended on how fast her case was resolved.

They strode out of the building and Luke grabbed her arm. "Ezzie, why didn't you tell me any of this yesterday?"

Because it isn't any of your business, she thought. *But he's your lawyer*. Crap. She should've told him, but it really wasn't relevant to her case. Though he probably could've helped her come up with a proposal or something.

She groaned. "I really didn't think I had to. Most of these people have been with me for the last three years. The rest have been with me since the bakery opened and I owe them an explanation and some kind of plan on how they're going to get paid. I understand the importance of their income and I just can't turn my back because everything I have built is going up in flames. So, either you go with me or I can leave you here and go by myself. Either way, you need to decide."

Still stubborn as ever. Nice to know some things never changed. Including that damn golden heart of hers. Always thinking of others before herself. Luke rubbed the top of his brow.

There were no good answers at the moment, but he also didn't have her full case file. The knowledge he had of the evidence the state had on her was limited, which didn't give a lot of options at the moment either. But he'd agreed to defend her to the best of his ability. Damn it. Okay. He could wing it with a few specifics from her.

"Fine. Let's go, but I need you to answer questions on the way there."

"Done." Ezzie took off down the sidewalk.

Luke followed after her. "Where exactly are we going?"

"The parking garage. With my bakery shut down, we can't meet there. I made arrangements to meet with my staff in a small conference room the coffee shop across from my bakery has available. Should take us about fifteen minutes to get there."

That was more detail than he'd asked for, but it was nice to have everything laid out all at once. It was easier to organize and execute actionable plans when all the pieces of the puzzle could be seen. "Guess that means I have fifteen minutes to learn what I can about your bakery."

"I don't know how useful I can be. I can offer more information on recipes than I can tell you regarding the business side of my bakery." She rounded the corner at the next block and walked into a multiple-level parking garage. She continued past the elevators and staircase and approached a blue four-door Jeep.

He raised an eyebrow. This wasn't the SUV she had last time they'd seen one another. She'd had an older black Jeep Wrangler. No way had he forgotten what that car looked like. Too many memories involved with that older Jeep. He proceeded around the newer Jeep—a Renegade. *Please don't let it be brand new.*

"How long ago did you get this?"

"I bought it two years ago. I didn't buy it right out. I do make monthly payments."

"Did you make a large down-payment?" He climbed into the passenger side.

There were a number of ways to embezzle and launder money, though he suspected the state didn't believe or couldn't link any evidence to this vehicle. Otherwise, it would've been seized with all of her other property.

Ezzie backed out and left the parking structure. "No. I only put down a couple thousand dollars. It was the third year the bakery had been open and most of the profit I made I reinvested into the bakery. I got the Renegade because it was more practical with Joey."

Good. One less thing he had to fret over. He'd make a mental note to confirm the vehicle was in favorable standing and it was entirely separate from the bakery, as well as check how she'd reinvested into the bakery itself. "Tell me about your initial investors."

"What do you want to know?"

"Names if you know them off hand, that would really be helpful. I also need to know what businesses they represented, how much they each invested, the amount of interest on the investment, when you were expected to pay it back, and when you actually paid it back."

It was a lot of information, but the more detailed she could be, the better prepared he would be. Not that it would offer a whole lot of help with the meeting they were heading toward. This wasn't the first time a client had decided to gather with their staff. Unfortunately, of all the meetings he'd attended, none had gone well. He wasn't inclined to believe this would be any different.

Ezzie blew out a deep breath. "The only names I can give you offhand are Matt's parents. They were my first investors. As for everything else, I have copies of the contracts at an office they let me use. Not just theirs, but for all of my investors. I believe most of them expected a pay-off around year three or four, but I managed to pay them all off in two."

"Is the office in your name?"

There was no way it could be. Anything in her name that had records would have been off limits as they would've been considered as part of the investigation. But if it wasn't in her name, well ... then it would depend on her record keeping. This could be exactly what they needed.

"No. It belongs to Matt's parents. It's what I used when I was first trying to get the bakery in working order. I just never really stopped using it, even after I hired an accountant."

Luke nodded. This was good. Fuck good, this was better than good. He could dive right in just the way he liked. "Then that's where we'll go after the meeting."

"About that. Before we get there, here." Ezzie dug around in her purse and handed him a compact.

"What's this for?"

"To try and cover that bruise on your jaw. I need you to be comforting, not intimidating."

He lowered the passenger side visor and eyed the deep purple mark on his jawline. It wasn't that bad. "I don't know that this will cover it."

"Maybe not entirely, but it should lessen its appearance."

"Then why put it on at all?" He was all for hiding the bruise. But not if it meant he had to wear make-up. Of any kind.

"Fine, then don't, but if anyone asks, you got into a fight with a thug who tried stealing your wallet."

"One, I don't know why anyone would ask. I don't know any of these people. Two, why would it be necessary for me to lie?"

His first statement made sense. His second, not so much. Even he knew it would be harder for anyone to trust in his word if they believed for one second he got into a stupid fight with his best friend. Or a well-deserved one.

"One, because people are nosey. Two, I prefer my staff see you as trustworthy."

Right, he needed to be viewed as *trustworthy*. Luke glanced from his reflection to the compact in his hand. "All right, I'll try the make-up."

Ezzie turned down the dirt road she had used for the last few years for the only sanctuary she had left. What the hell had she been thinking by calling that meeting? That had been the worst idea she'd ever had. Not only did it blow up in her face, but it divided her staff. A few of her long-term people understood she was in a difficult situation, but everyone else ... they were so angry. She didn't blame them.

The last thing she recalled saying replayed in her mind.

"I'm sorry. I don't know when you'll get paid or when you'll return to work." She paused and folded her hands. *"I'm really sorry. I just don't have any answers for you."*

The entire room erupted in an uproar.

She had never apologized to anyone that much in her life. Thank god, Luke had taken over from there. Although his presence hadn't been planned, she was so grateful he had gone along with her.

"Where are we at?"

"Part of the land that Matt's parents use for their vineyard. There's a small barn down this road that they rarely used. It was far enough away from everything that it wouldn't interfere with their day-to-day operations and it gave me space to think and organize. They've actually been really great to me over the years."

More so in the last week. They had covered her bail and even offered to pay for an attorney for her. She'd only accepted the first, but promised to pay them back every cent.

"Have they done anything else for you besides their initial investment?"

Smirking, she raised an eyebrow. He was kidding right? Didn't she just say they were heading to a barn that they allowed her to use as an office? "You mean aside from the obvious?"

"Yes. Anything else in your bakery. Did they help with any of the physical labor? Transport of goods? Anything like that."

"Oh, no. The funds they gave me covered building expenses, materials, and my first employee. Plus, I was able to pay Matt and Colin a small stipend for the work they did."

She'd been surprised at how far the money hadn't gone. Made her really dig into the business side of the bakery. She'd discovered it was the only way she'd ever be successful. She had put together a plan, which included her intention to expand after five years and presented it to multiple investment companies. In the end, she wound up with six additional investors after Matt's parents.

Ezzie smiled. Her bakery had taken off better than anyone had anticipated. Within two years, she'd paid all seven companies back with interest. After that, she didn't need any more investors. The bakery survived on its own profit.

"Who's Colin?"

Had she never said anything about Colin back when she and Luke dated? Hmm, maybe she hadn't. It wasn't as if she expected Matt's relationship with Colin to go the distance. None of her best friend's relationships ever lasted. His longest had been three months. Until Colin, that had become the standard. But not anymore.

"Matt's boyfriend."

Those are the most beautiful words I've ever heard. Luke exhaled. He didn't even realize he had held his breath. For a split second he thought Ezzie was about to say Colin was her boyfriend. Not that he would've been surprised if she had one. She was just as gorgeous as the first time they met all those years ago. Probably more so now.

Her mahogany locks were longer than he remembered. She wore it in the same ponytail he'd grown accustomed to, but it definitely hung further down her back than it had before. Her blue eyes brightened anytime she told him something about her bakery. Or when she spoke about food. Another thing that hadn't changed.

He really had to stop noticing these nuances. He was still supposed to be mad at her for lying about his son.

Ezzie slowed the Jeep and turned down another dirt road.

This barn was way off the beaten path. Then again, she always had a knack for finding places like that. Pushing the memories into the back recesses of his mind, Luke gazed out the passenger side window. From where they were, he could see the rows upon rows of vines covered in various shades of grapes. It was a never-ending sea of red and purple. He'd never toured a vineyard before, but from his vantage point it was pretty spectacular. The Jeep eased again and then stopped.

"We're here."

Luke shifted his eyes to the huge wooden building in front of them. It had to be at least twenty feet tall and thirty feet wide. It looked like it could easily hold a party with a hundred people, probably more. There was no real design to it though; it was pretty plain, not that he expected any differently. Of course, he didn't really have anything to compare it to. He'd never seen a barn before.

"You used that for an office?"

"Sure did." Ezzie got out of the SUV and headed for the doors.

He climbed out and clambered after her. As they approached the front of the building, he noticed a silver padlock on the barn doors like the kind used on gym lockers or bikes. Using a key from her pocket, Ezzie removed the padlock and slid one of the doors to the side.

Watching her cross the threshold, he observed the way she waltzed into the barn as if she owned it. Her entire demeanor changed. She stood a little taller, held her head a little higher, and carried herself with a little more confidence.

Luke regarded the inside of the barn. He could see how it affected her. It was like a fully functioning miniature house complete with kitchen, three picnic tables, office area and small den. A staircase on each side led up to a loft-style bedroom.

In the back corner, blueprints and yellow sticky notes were pinned to the wall. Plus, three or four metal cabinets sat on the ground below all that. With everything else that was there, she would've had no reason to leave. "I thought this was just your office."

"That's all I ever used it for. Sort of."

That was a half-ass answer if he ever heard one. What the hell was that supposed to mean? Had she slept there? Had she cooked there? Showered there?

"Sort of?"

"I was pregnant with Joey when I first started working on everything.

Some nights I ended up crashing here. It allowed me to get more work done. That all changed after he was born."

"As in you spent more time at home? Or you got less done?"

It made sense that their son uprooted her whole world. Of course, if he had known about Joey, he certainly would've been by her side to help. The years of his son's life he had missed out on; the first time he crawled, his first step, his first word—how could she have stolen all of that from him?

"Yeah, I spent more time at home, but I also had to figure out how to get tasks done around him. And I did."

He heard the unspoken words in her statement. Anyone with ears would've heard the same thing he had. *And I did it all without you.* She hadn't bothered to give him the chance to be a father. That was going to change, starting today. Shoving his hands in his pockets, Luke strode toward the desk.

"Let's get what we came for."

She was quite proud of all she had accomplished during her pregnancy. She'd only had about three months before Joey had been born to get the majority of the bakery up and running. It still required more after her son came into the world. She didn't sleep much for the first few months afterward, but it was worth it. Even if she was possibly losing it all, she wouldn't have changed anything in the last few years.

Ezzie pinched the bridge of her nose. Fuck, she seriously had to stop thinking like that. It was the entire reason Luke was there; to help her fight for everything she had built.

"There are a couple of empty boxes in the closet there. My early files are in the filing cabinets."

"Nothing's electronic?" Luke strolled past the desk onto the closet door.

"Just the last three years. When Jonathan took over all the bookkeeping, he insisted we upgrade to the latest technology. It worked fine for him because he understood all that, but me … I prefer something tangible."

She sat in the brown leather chair behind the large oak desk. Sitting there had been akin to getting flour all over her hands in her bakery's kitchen. Both places felt like home. Smiling, she booted up the computer.

"Who's that? Your manager?"

"No. Jonathan Burke. He's my accountant." Which reminded her, she still needed to go by his office. All of her phone calls and text messages over the weekend had gone unanswered. She didn't recall him having any vacation plans. He'd just … disappeared.

Luke returned with two empty boxes. "Have you spoken to him since your arrest?"

Shaking her head, she accessed the bookkeeping software he insisted they use and entered her password. *Password not valid?* How was that possible? She'd entered the correct password.

Hadn't she?

Focusing on the keyboard, she re-entered her password one character at a time and tried again. Ezzie frowned.

"What's wrong?" Luke walked around the desk and stood behind her.

Unable to immediately answer, she swallowed the saliva in the back of her throat to try and calm the butterflies flip-flopping in her belly. Why did he have to hover? This was why she'd given him a project, so he didn't invade her personal space.

Crikey, get it together! He should be able to stand wherever he wants. Focus on the task at hand.

"The software keeps telling me my password's wrong." *I know I didn't forget my password. Joey03!9.* This made no sense. She had used that same password for the last three years. It was the password she had used for college, her e-mail, her banking, and everything else. She tapped the keyboard and stared at the monitor. Maybe it had something to do with her arrest.

"Is this the only place you have the past records?"

"For the last three years, yes. No worries. Jonathan and I came up with a backup plan in case I ever got locked out." She removed a USB drive from the desk drawer to her right and plugged it into the hard drive. There had never been a reason to utilize Jonathan's secure password, but she was glad she had it. She had to get to the files.

Luke leaned forward resting one hand on the desk. "What just happened?"

"I ... I don't know."

Ezzie blinked. The hairs on the nape of her neck rose. Shivers crawled up her spine, but she wasn't certain if it was because Luke was standing so close to her or because of the blank screen staring her in the face.

Or both.

four

"I DON'T UNDERSTAND HOW this is even possible."

Makes two of us. The entire computer had crashed. They'd both attempted to restart the machine and it refused to turn on. He had a couple of ideas as to what occurred, but right now, it was just conjecture. Better they send the whole thing off to a computer technician he knew to get it checked out. Luke loaded the PC, hard drive, USB and all of the other components into a box.

"You're absolutely positive you've never utilized that USB before?"

"Yes." Ezzie shoved the last of the physical files she had into a bin.

"And you haven't heard anything from your accountant?" He really didn't want to share his thoughts with her. It had been plain to see over the last thirty minutes how much she trusted the guy, which only made him hope all of this could be blamed on an outside party.

He thought back on their arrival. The lock hadn't appeared to be jimmied, not that he'd scanned it either. Might be something to do on their way out.

"No, which is so weird. He's never without his phone. I figured I'd go by his office this afternoon."

An office was good. Less of a reason to involve the private investigator he and Nate had worked with in the past. There were a number of ways to handle this, but the most logical direction would be to make the trip to the accountant's office this morning. Then he and Ezzie could decide on next steps. If nothing else, they had at least two years' worth of documentation to review and it gave him a starting point. It may not be everything he preferred to have access to, but it was better than nothing.

"Why don't we go by his office on our way back to the city?"

"Are you sure?"

"Yes. That way if he's there, then he and I can sit down and talk."

Closing up the box, Luke inwardly sighed. If this accountant of hers wasn't directly connected to the embezzlement, then he had to know who was responsible. There was no way this Jonathan fellow had done her bookkeeping for three years without detecting any suspicious activity. Shit. He was going to have to get a forensic accountant to go over all her books to

Then again, maybe not. He understood the financial particulars of running a business and grasped enough information to dig out what typically didn't belong. Still, this was Ezzie's life on the line. They'd comb through the accounting records together, but he'd get a forensic accountant to dig through everything too.

His gaze settled on her face. Slowly his eyes dropped lower and focused on her mouth. Her normal pouty lips pressed into a thin line. He hated to see her so frustrated. What could he do to make her smile return? What had he done in the past—

No, he couldn't do that. He was her lawyer.

He wouldn't take any chances when it came to her.

Not one.

"Are you okay?"

Shit! He'd been staring. He had to stop that. It was no way to behave around a client, even if that client happened to be his beautiful ex-girlfriend. He had to remind himself of that. Would probably help if he quit thinking about her as beautiful … maybe even his ex-girlfriend. He had to lock her in the role of client. And nothing more.

Luke picked up the box. "Yeah. Let's go."

They had to postpone their visit to her accountant's office until tomorrow. Her son would be getting out of school soon. With it being Pre-K, he was in school four hours a day for four days out of the week. He'd normally go to the babysitter's until around 5 P.M., and then she'd pick up him on her way home from the bakery. It was another thing on the list that she could no longer afford with her accounts frozen. This all just needed to get resolved, quickly.

Ezzie unlocked the door to her apartment and lugged one of the two boxes filled with her early files into the dining room. She dropped her load onto the dining room table. "We can work here for a little bit."

Following her example, Luke off-loaded the box he'd brought up. "If we have to move everything to my hotel suite after the hearing tomorrow morning, then we can certainly do that."

"Do you think it would be necessary?" Closing the front door, she hung her purse up on the nearby rack. *Please let him say no.* Being alone … in a hotel room with him … she couldn't think of a worse idea. *Sure, you can.* After all, she could sleep with him. "Shut up!"

"What did I say?"

Shit. She hadn't meant to say that out loud. Ezzie massaged her temples. She had to get the hell out of her own head. Otherwise, she was really going to say something she regretted. "Sorry. Nothing. We can move if need be."

"It might be easier on both of us. It'll come down to the evidence the prosecutor's office has against you and our ability to gain access to your books for the last three years."

Why did he have to be so logical about it? She had no argument against a valid point. A quick glance at the clock on the wall told her she had to get lunch going. Pausing midway to the kitchen, she raised an eyebrow. "Wait a minute. Why would we need both?"

"Embezzlement charges can be difficult to prove unless a sting of some kind has been executed. That means the only way they could have sufficient evidence against you is if someone provided it to them. This would be advantageous to us in your case. We want both sets so that we can easily identify discrepancies."

She opened her mouth and shut it. The way he explained all of that made it sound like he believed someone she knew set her up. No way. Not even possible. She had worked with all of her people for years and trusted every single one of them.

"Do you honestly think—"

The front door flew open.

Her son dropped his backpack on the floor, ran down the hallway and hollered a "hello" in passing.

Matt stepped through the door after Joey took off inside. The kid had been bouncing around the elevator the entire ride up. Guess Mother Nature—

He stopped in the doorway. Shit. He eyed the front door from his periphery. Was it too late to turn around and exit? Catching a glimpse of the steam pouring out Luke's ears, he'd go with yes. Option two it was; pretend like they had never met.

Smiling, he shut the door. "Hey Ezzie, you're home earlier than I anticipated."

"Yeah. I figured it was best I was here when Joey got home."

"I get that, but if you need me to, I can always take him to my place."

Then he'd definitely avoid her ex-boyfriend, which sounded like an awesome idea. It would reduce the likelihood of her finding out about his involvement in their earlier separation to almost zero. Unless, of course, she'd been told. Matt studied the facial features of Ezzie's ex. He could see the determination behind those brown eyes of his, but there was something else. What though? And what was the determination about?

"I may have you do that over the next few days." Ezzie paused and peeked down the hallway, then lowered her voice. "I'm pretty sure we'll have a lot of work to do on the case."

This was the perfect opportunity to introduce himself. She hadn't done it yet and clearly her ex was waiting to see what he would do. "We?"

He didn't bother to wait on Ezzie to pick up on the term, not that it was necessary. Grinning, Matt offered his hand to Luke. "You must be the lawyer I've heard so much about. I'm Matt."

"Oh god. I'm sorry. I forgot you guys haven't met. Luke, Matt. Matt, Luke."

Was this douche bag seriously holding his hand out for a handshake? As if they hadn't met before? Luke regarded Ezzie. She truly believed everything she'd said. How did she not know?

He returned his attention to the shithead that had stood between them a few years ago. If there was one thing he could say law school taught him, beside the law, was how to spot liars. Staring into Matt's eyes, it all made sense.

His ex-girlfriend didn't know he had shown up on her doorstep because she hadn't been told. All right, if that was the way this guy wanted to play it, he'd go along with it.

For now. Standing, Luke placed his hand in the one that had been extended and shook it tightly. "Right. Ez's best friend. How could I forget?"

"Yep, that's me."

"Good to meet you."

Noting the way Matt cringed, he released his hand. Yeah, it had been a spiteful move, but at least this way Ezzie's so-called best friend knew who was in control. The only reason he didn't utter one word about what had gone on back then was his son. If he initiated a fight, he'd lose on a chance to spend time with his son and he refused to do that.

"You too. Well, if you don't need me, I'll just head home." He turned toward the door.

"Thanks, Matt. I appreciate you getting Joey for me." Ezzie walked him out of the apartment.

At least he didn't have to worry about his son being around that dickhead for the rest of the afternoon. Not that it would make a difference if he wound up working for hours on end. Luke sized up the two boxes of files in front of him. It would take them a while to go through all the documentation collected. He rubbed the back of his neck.

"Whatcha lookin' at, Mr. Luke?" Joey asked.

He loathed that term. He liked it better when his son called him uncle. It may not have been his real role, but it was closer than "mister." He'd have to talk to Ezzie about that. Somewhere in the midst of preparing for her defense, they'd have to decide when to come clean with their son.

Luke inhaled a deep breath and quietly exhaled. "Your mom was nice enough to let me bring some of my work over."

"That doesn't sound very fun."

"Well, I think it is, but that's because I like helping good people defeat the bad guys."

It wasn't his usual description, but he was talking to a four-year-old and it seemed appropriate. Minus the bad guys part.

"That sounds like what my dad does. He—"

Ezzie clapped her hands together. "Who's ready for lunch?"

"Oh, me!" Joey jumped up and down with his hand in the air.

His dad? Luke blinked. He didn't move from the dining room table as Ezzie strolled past him into the kitchen. He watched as she went about gathering mustard, meat and cheese from the refrigerator; bread from the counter; a knife from a drawer.

She flitted around without giving away any clue that she'd heard what their son told him. His son had said once before that he'd been told stories, but he hadn't detailed or shared any of the stories. Joey had even described his father as being like a superhero.

Nothing else had been obtained. Luke shifted his gaze from Ezzie to Joey.

Did his son know who he was?

Did his son … know him?

Maybe he'd heard his son all wrong.

He had to have imagined it all.

Or had he actually heard him?

There had been so many papers for them to go through. Ezzie dragged the race-car comforter and top sheet aside. She had never been happier to cook dinner and get her son ready for bed. She hadn't planned for Luke to stay for dinner, but her son insisted. With the two of them pleading with her like a team, she'd been unable to resist and agreed.

Not that it had been as bad as she thought it would be. As long as no one looked too closely at the glances she kept stealing of Luke. Every time she caught a glimpse of him all she saw were the things she loved about him. The slight smile he wore whenever he rambled some random history fact. Or the way he beamed as their son shared everything, he had done in school that day. Even how Luke's eyes lit up with each bite of food he swallowed like it was that first taste of water on a hot summer's day.

Those nuances of his flooded her brain with memories of their time together, which was the last thing she needed to be thinking about. His entire purpose for being there was to help her with her case. Nothing more. Who was she kidding? He'd indicated his readiness to discuss how they would handle arrangements with her son. She wasn't the least bit prepared.

"All done." Dressed in race car PJs, Joey waltzed into the bedroom.

Ezzie bent down to her son's height. "Let me smell."

He exhaled a breath in her face; fresh and minty.

If she didn't check, he wouldn't brush his teeth. She'd learned that the hard way. Smiling, she straightened and gestured to his bed. "Get in."

"Hey Mommy, did you know Mr. Luke does work like my daddy?" He climbed into his bed.

Hell, how was she supposed to answer that? *Of course, he does because he is your father.* Yeah, that would go over well. It wasn't like she could disregard the question. She had to come up with something. She tucked the covers around him, swept some of his hair back and brushed a gentle kiss against his forehead. "Oh yeah?"

"Yep. He does. Mommy? Will you tell me about one of Daddy's rescues?"

Her son hadn't asked for a story in over a month. Last time he'd claimed to be too old for them. As much as she loathed the idea of telling her son a story about his father with his father in the house, she'd give him a story while she still could. She knew Luke would do everything in his power to save her, but she wasn't positive it would be enough.

Sitting on the edge of the bed, Ezzie smiled. "There was this builder who had slaved away for many, many months on a really tall building. It reached all the way to the sky. Then one day the evil owner came by to check on his progress. As he was looking into the different rooms, a heavy stack fell on him and he got hurt. He yelled at the builder and said it was all his fault; that he used way too much straw when he should've used brick. He told the builder he had to take it all apart and do the whole building all over again. That's when your dad swooped in to save the day."

Listening in to the bedtime story being told, Luke propped up against the wall outside his son's bedroom. He recalled that case. It was one of the first cases he'd ever worked. It had been a property owner suing the construction company who'd done the building repairs. How had Ezzie known about that? Had she been following his career?

"With his cape flapping in the wind, he landed right in front of the evil owner and he showed him pictures that revealed exactly what the owner had done. The owner's eyes widened and he begged your dad to forgive him."

He smirked. That was close to the truth. He'd found video footage that exposed the owner destroying the work that the construction company had done, which is what caused one of the beams in the wall to fall. The owner wound up paying out double the normal cost to the construction company for the repairs completed, plus his company's fees.

"Your dad told him to apologize to the builder. The owner did, and then he ran off, never to bother the builder again."

"He saved the builder," Joey said.

"Yes, he did. Good night, baby."

"Good night, Mommy."

Ezzie shuffled backward out of the bedroom and shut the door most of the way.

That had been a nice ending. About as good as how that case had ended. She had a way with retelling his cases. Had she turned all of them into a bedtime story for their son? Would explain what his son had said earlier about his work.

"That was really sweet."

Clutching her chest, she jerked back. "Crikey. You scared the shit out of me."

"I'm sorry. That wasn't my intention. I just like the way you told that story. How did you come up with it?"

Why had he asked her that? *That's easy. You want her to admit she's been checking on you.* Luke held back the internal groan. His reasoning shouldn't surprise him. She'd been on his mind a lot over the years. He wanted to know she'd thought about him too.

"I read it somewhere." Strolling past him, she headed toward the living room.

"A newspaper, perhaps?"

He followed after her. All she had to do was admit she'd been keeping tabs on him. It shouldn't be hard … or any harder than him fessing up about his trip to her old apartment, which included his previous meeting with her best friend.

Snatching a kitchen towel from the counter, Ezzie sighed. "Yes, I read it in a paper. Yes, I use your court cases as bedtime stories. I had to do something."

Narrowing his eyes, Luke crossed his arms. Not quite the explanation he had hoped for and definitely not what he longed to hear.

He shook his head. "You could've told me about him. That would've been the thing to do."

She faced him. "I tried that before he was born, but you never answered. By the time he came around, I decided maybe it was best you didn't know. You could finish college without us weighing you down."

"What about after college? I did graduate, you know." He hadn't heard from her at all. Whatever method she'd used to contact him had failed miserably.

"I'm well aware of that, but to answer your question, by that time…" Ezzie paused. She got this remorseful look in her eyes and turned away. "… by then I didn't know what to say."

Luke rubbed his forehead with his thumb. There were a million ways she could've said something. *Hey Luke, I know we haven't seen each other in a couple of years, but guess what, you're a dad. Or, hey Luke, you've won the lottery and now you're a father. Or…*

None of those sounded viable.

"So, instead of telling me about our son, you chose to tell him stories about me?"

"I had no choice. Joey started asking questions. I had to come up with something." Ezzie frowned. Her heart had broken the first time her son had mentioned other kids having a daddy. Not because he had asked about his own, but because he seemed so sad and lost. She'd made it her mission since then to do whatever it took for him to learn about his father.

"But my court cases as bedtime stories?"

Sort of. She had been seeking out information regarding the success of his career before that had even come up. It reassured her she'd made the right decision to leave Luke's graduation ceremony. Then one night after her son had made inquiries, the story she told tonight came out. She refused to tell him that. The how shouldn't be important.

"Yeah, and he likes them."

"I think that's a testament to how well you recount the story. Almost makes me sound like a hero."

"That's you, Luke. You're good at what you do. I've never doubted that."

No matter what they had gone through, that remained true. Ezzie lifted her gaze to those deep-set eyes of his. If he accepted nothing else from her as truth, she hoped he accepted that. Her faith in his ability to become a great lawyer had never deterred.

Luke stood there in silence. His eyes flickered over her face. "You really mean that?"

Since the day he'd shared his desire to go into law school. Every case he won reaffirmed what she had known all along. "I've always believed in you. That's part of what made keeping Joey from you so hard. As much as I knew the kind of the lawyer you'd become, I also knew you'd be a great dad."

His eyebrows knitted together.

She hadn't meant to admit all of that. But it felt good to get all of it off her chest. It was all true. With everything she'd kept from Luke, he deserved some honesty.

Ezzie bit her bottom lip. "I'm sorry I didn't tell you about Joey, but I can't change the past. All I can do now is try to figure out how to tell him who you are and ensure you're a part of his life."

"I'd like that. To be a part of his life."

Telling her son an acceptable truth would be where she had to start. That wasn't true. She had to ascertain that truth first.

Ezzie nodded. "Okay. I'll find a way to tell him and we'll come to some arrangements. Just, give me some time."

"I can do that."

There was a knock on the door to his hotel suite. Luke eyed the time on his Rolex. It couldn't be Ezzie. She wasn't due to pick him up for another thirty minutes. He got up from the California law books splayed open on the coffee table and answered the door.

"Ezzie? What are you doing here?"

"I know you told me seven-thirty, but as I was doing my make-up, I remembered the bruise on your face."

"Ugh."

Yeah, because it had done wonders the day before. He rolled his eyes and returned to the law books he'd been reading.

Ezzie closed the door and accompanied him. "Yes, I know, yesterday morning was a disaster, but I'm fully prepared today. I have all the necessary tools to cover that bad boy up."

It shouldn't matter a small portion of his face resembled the color of a plum. It was healing, slowly. He looked over at her and cocked an eyebrow at the pink case in her hand. "What is that?"

"It's a make-up case."

"Since when did you get one of those?"

He had never seen her wear much make-up. Even now, she hardly had any on. A little bit of gray eye shadow, which made the blue in her eyes pop. Maybe some of that stuff that goes on the lashes, although hers were long enough without it. And a touch of red lipstick.

"Um, a little over two years ago." She set her case down on the coffee table and flipped the lid.

"Why? You've never used most of that gunk."

Ezzie pulled out a tube-like container and twisted it free. "I still don't, but your son happens to like buying it for me for Christmas. Now, look at the T.V."

"How is that even possible? He's four." Luke frowned. He didn't like this, but he turned his head as instructed.

"A couple of years ago, Matt took him Christmas shopping for me. All he did was let Joey point out what he wanted to get me. Granted, they were in Sephora, but I ended up with most of what you see here and it's become a tradition. So, I use it." She streaked some of the tan glob on his face.

He flinched. He meant to ice his jaw when he'd gotten back last night, but he'd been numb to the pain.

"Sorry. Is this still sore?" Ezzie stroked his jawline.

His eyelids folded over his eyes. If she kept on touching him, he wasn't going to feel anything. The sensation of her fingers against his chin made his toes tingle. "Not much."

"I'll be gentle."

His body hummed beneath the tender touch. Luke relished the sensation. Her brother hadn't done as much damage as he could have. The bruises on his abs and face would heal; he was more concerned with the damage done to his relationship with his best friend. It was almost like what he'd done to his relationship with Ezzie. At one point, he thought it had been irrevocable, but with the way she was being so considerate with his jaw … made him think otherwise.

Luke couldn't see her move, but he could hear and feel every small step. She had gone from the stick gook to a cold, wet glob, then something clicked and whatever she was using was brushed on his face.

"Done. Take a look."

Damn. That was over way too soon. Luke opened his eyes and checked out his reflection. He tilted his head this way and that. It wasn't perfect, but the bruise was barely visible. "Wow. That's pretty amazing, Ez."

"All in a day's work. Now, what do you say we get this over with?"

He watched as Ezzie put the make-up case back together. The feel of her fingers on his cheek lingered. She was just as beautiful as ever. He shouldn't notice the way her black slacks hugged her ass or how they elongated her already long legs. Or how her mahogany hair swayed with each movement. Or how the red suit jacket made her skin stand out.

But he did.

Luke stood and leered at her through hooded eyes. His heart pounded in his chest. Dear god, he wanted her.

Ezzie's sparkling blue eyes lifted to his. Cupping his jaw with her fingers, she brushed her thumb gently across the covered bruise. "I still can't believe Nate hit you."

He leaned into her hand. Whatever pain he'd felt before dissipated as if it had never been there. "I deserved it."

"No, you didn't." She caressed his cheek.

Don't do it. Just walk away, Luke thought. But he couldn't. Tucking a few wisps of her hair behind her ear, Luke pressed his lips to hers.

Fuck! Her lips were as soft as they'd always been. They still tasted like strawberries; his favorite flavor. *This is a bad idea. You need to—*

Her arms linked around his neck and she deepened the kiss.

Using his tongue, Luke stroked her bottom lip.

Ezzie moaned and their tongues dueled fast and furious.

God, this felt so good. This was all wrong, but he couldn't help himself. He wrapped an arm around her waist and squeezed.

She shoved him off her. Her hand flew to her mouth.

Quietly panting, they gawked at one another. *Fuck.* What had he done? Luke swallowed. Shit, shit, shit.

"I'm sorry. I don't know what came over me."

"We can't do that. You're my lawyer." Shaking her head, she scooped up the make-up case.

"God, Ez—"

"Let's just go."

"I told you this would be quick and painless."

Luke held the courtroom door open for Ezzie. Getting the motion allowing him to represent her granted had been a one-on-one fist fight compared to the battle that lay in front of them. He should have copies of the evidence the prosecutor had against her in matter of hours. Now if they could obtain the rest of her logs, he'd have a leg to stand on.

He drank in the sight of her as she removed the red suit jacket she had on. It complemented her entire outfit well. She was dressed in a pair of black slacks with a black and white striped sleeveless silk blouse. A simple pair of diamond studs completed the look. What really got him though was the way she'd worn her hair down. He'd had to stop himself from reaching out and running his fingers through it several times.

You're her lawyer had become the worst kind of broken record he'd ever heard and it was only in his own head. Yet he had to keep reminding himself of that. *Focus, jackass.*

Throwing her hair up in a ponytail, she headed down the steps of the courthouse. "Yeah, but we're nowhere near the whole thing being over and done."

"That's why we focus on one step at a time. We're past the first hurdle. Now, we move onto your accountant. We'll swing by his office on the way back to the hotel and see what we can find. That'll keep us moving in the right direction."

Luke descended the cement staircase. He'd taken many stairs going in and out of a number of courthouses, but none of them had been as important as this one. In less than a week, they would return and he'd fight for a life that mattered a lot to him. He didn't need to win just for Ezzie, but for their son as well.

"I guess so."

Luke frowned. She had been off a little all morning, ever since she'd finished covering the bruise. It couldn't be due to the kiss they shared earlier. No. There had to be something more going on here.

He grasped the crook of her elbow. "Hey, are you okay with all this? You can talk to me."

His grip prevented her from continuing on to the lot where she had parked. Ezzie bit the inside of her cheek. Yeah, she could trust him, but did she want to be entirely honest with him about what she was feeling? How small and helpless all of this made her feel? She glanced back at the courthouse. Standing beside him in front of the judge made her fully aware of all she had to lose.

Being forced to close her bakery had been a nightmare, but it could be re-opened. The possibility of her customers finding out about her arrest slapped her down another notch, but reputations could be rebuilt. Dragging her son through this with the possibility of never seeing him grow up … that she couldn't handle. Until she had no choice.

She turned back to Luke. "I'm scared."

"Of what?"

"That we'll fail and I'll lose Joey. I couldn't breathe if I didn't have my little boy in my life."

That might be a bit on the dramatic side, but this was her son they were talking about. That's not right. This was *their* son. Yeah, if they couldn't prove her innocence, she'd wind up in jail, but would their son still be taken care of?

Luke clutched her shoulders and enfolded her in his arms. He tucked her head beneath his chin. "Hey, none of that. We aren't going to fail. You have me and my entire team on your side. We're going to do whatever it takes to get you out of this mess. I promise."

She enveloped her arms around his back. Every fiber in her body lit up and warmed her from the inside out. It had been a while since she'd been held like this, but they couldn't stay this way for too long. The emotional repercussions would be too much for them to deal with. Besides, she had to think about their son.

A promise was nice, but it wasn't a guarantee. They were a long way away from that. Releasing her grip, she extracted herself from the cradle of his arms. Ezzie stared at Luke for a moment. All she could see was their son's face in his, but that told her exactly what needed to be done if they lost her case.

"If we don't succeed, I need you to do something for me. I need you to take Joey."

Luke frowned. The drive to her accountant's office had been quiet. He hadn't been able to bring himself to even remotely discuss her request. He didn't want to consider the possibility of raising their son without her. Let alone how they'd go about telling their son he was his father. All he kept seeing in his head was some kind of bad Luke Skywalker scene.

At least they were at her accountant's building, which gave him something else to fixate on. He glanced up at the glass building. Despite its small size, it screamed pretentious. God, he hoped this guy wasn't the uptight, know-it-all kind. "How did you meet this guy anyway?"

"Would you believe we bumped into each other at the coffee house across the street from my bakery?"

"Please tell me you're joking." The way her eyes steeled told him she had told him the complete truth. It bothered him on some deep level that he wasn't prepared to explore. Luke rubbed the nape of his neck and nodded.

"I know it's a total cliché, but that's what happened. I was on my way out; he was coming in and I knocked into him. I spilled my coffee all over the floor. He bought me a new cup and we talked."

It really was a total cliché, but that wasn't what troubled him. Ezzie was an amazing and stunning woman, he wouldn't be surprised to find out she had dated in the last five years or that multiple guys had hit on her. What bugged him was the coincidence. They weren't anywhere near her bakery. What person goes out of their way for coffee at a shop that is nowhere near their place of business?

"Did he tell you then that he was an accountant?"

"Yeah. We set up a meeting for the following day and things went from there."

"You checked this guy out, right? I mean, checked on his credentials."

Her story gave him a sense of déjà vu. A friend of his had represented a young woman who had been the mark of a Ponzi scheme. She had been targeted by the perpetrator in almost the same way Ezzie had been when it came to this so-called accountant. The elevator doors opened and they got on.

"I did my due diligence, researched him online and verified his credentials with the ACCA."

Luke swallowed the sigh that was desperate to escape. The ACCA wasn't the AICPA and that had been the one verification he'd been gunning for, but maybe he was wrong about this whole thing. Maybe they'd get to the fifth floor, head into this accountant's office and all the red flags would turn out to be just in his imagination.

The elevator dinged and the doors parted for them. They got off and walked across the foyer to a frosted glass door.

Ezzie pulled on the handle, but the door didn't budge. She yanked again, but the door still didn't move.

"That's weird. He's always here during the day."

This isn't good. God, please, please let me be wrong. There was an explanation. It would be great if it wasn't the one, he'd been thinking all along. He eyeballed the hours listed clear as day to the left of the door.

"Have you tried calling him? Maybe he's out to lunch or he's meeting with a client offsite."

"I called him before we left the courthouse, but he didn't answer. You could be right though."

Which was exactly why she had planned ahead. Ezzie dug her keys out of her pocket. The government may have shut down her bakery, but they hadn't taken away her keys, which just so happened to include a set to her accountant's office.

"What are you doing?"

"I have a key."

Snapping an arm out, Luke pushed her hand away from the door. "How do you have a key?"

Oh, how do I answer that? Ezzie thought.

It hadn't been her wisest idea, but Matt had made some valid points that she hadn't been able to ignore. She never wanted to fire her accountant, though maybe if she had she wouldn't be where she stood. She bit her bottom lip. Could she plead the fifth with her own lawyer?

"I think it's best I don't answer that."

"Tell me. As long as you didn't steal it, there shouldn't be a problem."

"Well, that's not the word I would use. I would say borrowed." So, she might have secretly obtained a copy of the key. Given the circumstances, it appeared to be necessary, although she'd never expected to use it.

"Oh hell. Here I thought things couldn't get any worse."

Oh, it can definitely get worse. Disregarding his latter statement, Ezzie held up the key. "Do you want me to use it or not?"

Luke hung his head. "I can't believe I'm going to say this, but go ahead."

"Thank you."

With that out of the way, she unlocked the door and tugged it open. An alarm to her left beeped. Without missing a beat, Ezzie punched in a code and the alarm system shut off. That she had to get from Jonathan's assistant. It had been in her desk. The young woman had been pretty, but had the memory of a chimp.

Ezzie turned around and noticed the empty room. The couches in the waiting area that she had sat on multiple times were no longer there. Neither was the coffee table with all the horrible magazines she'd been forced to read during those time she waited. Where had they gone? Was

Jonathan rearranging?

Her gaze shifted to the receptionist desk against the back wall. She blinked. The desk was gone too! Her eyes bounced from one side of the room to the other and she was surrounded by nothing but empty walls. Where was everything? Had the place been robbed?

That didn't make any sense. Who would break into an accountant's office and steal … furniture? Plus, the alarm had been on. What thief would consider turning the alarm back on after breaking in? What other option…

Her eyes widened and her palms bloomed with sweat. No, no, no, no! She raced down the hallway that led to Jonathan's office. None of the other offices had ever been filled. They had sat vacant the entire three years she had known him.

Not pausing for a second, she threw open the door to his corner office and saw more empty space. No desk, no filing cabinets, no chairs. No matter which direction she looked there was nothing in the office.

Her lungs tightened and her breaths came out in heavy spurts. Ezzie stared, wide-eyed, at all the bareness in front of her. This couldn't be happening. This had to be a bad dream.

But it wasn't.

Everything in the office was all … gone.

five

EZZIE STARED AT THE PAPERWORK in front of her, but she hadn't been able to read a single line. The vacancy of her accountant's office didn't sit well with her. She hadn't even been able to drive from there back to Luke's hotel. Good thing he'd learned how to navigate the streets of Los Angeles because she'd done nothing but sat there quietly. That hadn't changed when he'd gone downstairs to get the evidence files they were reviewing.

None of them made any sense thus far, though it would probably help if she actually comprehended any of the words on the paper. Instead, her mind kept going back to the brief conversation with the building's landlord. According to him, Jonathan had emptied his office Tuesday afternoon. She hadn't even been arrested yet!

It completely ruined her theory that the place had been robbed. Then again, it was a ridiculous thought anyhow. Who'd want to steal office furniture? Hanging her head, she interlaced her fingers at the nape of her neck. She was so confused.

Fingers snapped in her face.

She jerked back. Letting out a deep breath, Ezzie narrowed her eyes. "Crikey. Why do you insist on scaring the shit out of me?"

"Normally I'd say because it's fun, but I've been trying to get your attention for the last five minutes." Luke smirked.

"I'm sorry. I guess my brain is a little hyper-focused right now."

That was the understatement of the century. Her mind had been going around in circles trying to identify what she'd missed. There had to have been something she didn't see. Otherwise, she wouldn't be sitting on the floor of a hotel room with her ex-boyfriend combing through evidence stacked against her while her so-called accountant had up and disappeared.

Setting the paperwork aside, he took her hand in his own. "Listen to me. None of this is your fault. You couldn't have foreseen any of this."

"But I feel like I should have. Matt even told me he didn't get good vibes from Jonathan and they only met twice. I got with him multiples times a week for three years and not once did I feel like I couldn't trust him. What does that say about me?"

"That you see the good in people. That you give them the benefit of the doubt, whether they deserve it or not. It's what you did with me and I suspect it wasn't any different with this guy."

"That's not a fair comparison. You're nothing alike." And she had never been attracted to Jonathan. He'd been a scrawny guy and often wore business suits she swore would swallow him. It seemed as if he'd tried too hard to fit into his father's shoes. Luke was nothing like that.

Never mind the fact that every suit she'd ever seen him wear had been perfectly trimmed to his broad shoulders, sculpted arms, tight abs, and lean legs. The physicality of his appearance was only half the package. He had a good heart, regularly put others before himself, and was quite passionate about his work.

"All I'm saying is that you wanted to believe in him, so you did. You can't fault yourself for that."

"So I shouldn't feel like a fool?"

"No. I think you should be upset that this guy played you, which you then use to find a way out of this mess, while letting my private investigator work on locating Jonathan Burke."

Ezzie nodded. That sounded like a good plan to her, though she kind of hoped they came across the piece-of-shit. She'd show him she wasn't the kind of woman you screwed over.

"Okay. Let's get back to work."

"Then look over this contract. Is this one of the investors you worked with?" Luke held out the paperwork he had in his hand.

Taking the documentation from him, she scanned the name of the company: J.J. Banks Investment Company. Who the hell was that? She flipped through the rest of the contract and examined the date and signature lines.

"No. I don't recognize this company, but this kind of looks like my signature."

"Kind of?"

"See this curlicue at the top of the 'E,' I don't do that. And the way the 'n' and the 'o' are connected, I don't do that either."

It was small, but it was better than nothing. Something that proved she didn't sign this contract, which likely applied to any of the others outside her original investors.

"That's good. I know a writing expert we can reach out to, have the contracts with your actual signature compared to the others. I'll have my P.I. see if these companies have video footage. We might be able to use that to prove you were never even there." He hopped to his feet and snagged his cell phone off the bed.

"It definitely won't show me there. I remember this date. This is the last time Beverly was in town."

The words escaped her mouth before she had time to realize what she'd said. Or that she'd said it out loud. Shit. Had she really just inadvertently revealed a secret she swore to take to her gave? Ezzie glanced at Luke. By the look on his face, she'd go with *yes*.

Did she just use my mother's name? Nope. He had to have dreamt it because there was no way his mother had come to Los Angeles, visited with his ex-girlfriend without so much as once mentioning his son's existence. No possible way his mother would keep a secret from him, let alone something that important.

Luke zeroed in on the panic in Ezzie's eyes. "Son of a bitch! You mean to tell me that *my* mother knew about my son?"

"She might have."

"That is a yes or no question! There is no might, just yes or no. Did my mother know about Joey?" God help his mother if she did. It was bad enough Ezzie had kept his son from him, but his mother too?

She sighed. "Yes, Beverly knew."

There had to be an explanation, like maybe she'd found out recently. It was possible. His mother had befriended Ezzie over the years. Or … or … he had no other options. It was the only plausible excuse. That he could handle.

Luke inhaled and exhaled a few deep breaths. "How long?"

"How long what?"

"How long did she know?" he practically screamed.

Damn it. Ezzie wasn't stupid, but her inability to answer him straight was trying his nerves. Was she aiming to pull him into an argument he didn't want any part of? All he wanted was answers, which sure as hell wasn't too much to ask.

"Since before he was born. Please, don't be upset with your mother. She only did as I asked."

His mother knew while Ezzie was pregnant. Tightening his grip on his cell phone, Luke swallowed. It took every ounce of control he had not to yell. The two most important women in his life lied to him. And not a minor lie, a big lie.

"Four years, Ez. You stole four years from me. That doesn't count all the things I would've been able to experience throughout your pregnancy. I've missed all of it because you and my mother decided you knew what was best for me."

"You can't blame her for this. She didn't decide anything."

"Bullshit! No matter what you asked of her, she didn't have to abide by any of it. And she did!"

Jabbing his finger in her face, he balled up his fist. He had to get out of there. Anything that came out of his mouth was going to be out of pure anger. They had way too much to accomplish for him to spout something he'd regret later. Snatching a key card off the dresser, Luke stormed off.

He hadn't worn a path around the hotel yet, but if he kept walking around like this, he just might. At this point, he'd calmed down enough to talk to Ezzie and call his mother. That was a must. Luke rode the elevator back up to his floor and headed to his room. He opened the door to his hotel suite and paused in the doorway.

From where he stood, he could see a stack of papers on the desk, but nothing else. But if he had to guess, Ezzie was gone. Letting the door close behind him, he crossed the living room area to the desk. A note had been neatly placed atop the stack of papers.

Luke,

These are all the contracts with investment companies I don't recognize. It appears to be five in total. I'm sorry about earlier, but I couldn't keep waiting. I had to get Joey. We'll talk later.

Ezzie

Dragging a hand down his face, he strolled into the connecting bedroom and stopped at the mini-refrigerator. Eyeballing the time on his Rolex, he scanned the various mini-bottles of liquor on top of the refrigerator. He'd been gone longer than he expected. Of course, it had taken way more time than usual for him to return to a semi-normal state of control.

No good liquor in the minibar. Great.

He'd have to settle for what was there and have it stocked properly later. Turning a glass over, he reached into the ice bucket and scooped out a few ice cubes that hadn't melted yet. Luke dropped them in the glass and emptied a tiny bottle of Jack Daniels into it. Taking a sip of the Jack, he sat in a nearby chair and dug his cell phone out of his pocket.

He typically called his mother once a week, but they hadn't spoken in close to two. His last case had taken up a lot of his time, then he found out about his son and he hadn't quite come up with a way to tell his parents. If his mother knew, did it mean his father did too? He groaned and took another sip of the Jack. The gold liquid didn't burn all that much. He had really hoped it would be like fire going down the back of his throat. It would distract him from the emotional pain coursing through his veins.

Pulling up his mother's contact information, he Face-timed her.

The line rang twice and she picked up. "Hi, sweetie. I was beginning to—what's wrong?"

"How could you not tell me?" He didn't mean for the question to pop out like that, but regular pleasantries were overrated. The last two hours of walking around in circles had led him to one conclusion: he required answers.

"What are you—"

"Cut the crap, Mom! I know I have a son. What I want to know is how you couldn't find a way to tell me?"

With the drink in his hand, Luke thrust his finger at his mother. It didn't seem like an unreasonable request. In some odd way, he partially understood Ezzie's position, but it still didn't change the fact he deserved to know about his progeny. But his mother ... he was sure as hell she didn't have a decent excuse.

"Oh, sweetie." His mother sighed.

"That's not an answer!"

Her eyes narrowed and her entire face screwed up. "Lucas Daniel Jonnihan, I understand you are upset, but you will not take that tone with me. I am still your mother."

"Then tell me the truth."

Upset didn't begin to describe how he felt. Betrayed was a more accurate word. His relationship with his mother had been strong growing up. She may not have been the one he went to when it came to relationship problems, but the woman could spot them a mile away and often had the right answer. All that trust had been slammed in a trunk and tossed in a river the second he found out she lied about his son.

"I wanted to tell you, many times, though I could never bring myself to do it."

What kind of excuse was that? Aside from lousy, it offered no information whatsoever. It was like a client pleading "not guilty," but him with no plan or way to back it up. Luke frowned. His mother had to give him more.

"Why? Why couldn't you do it?"

"Every time I had decided that would be the call, that would be the time I would tell you, you would mention a test you had to study for or a paper you had to work on and all I could hear were my conversations with Esmeralda. She believed if you found out about Joseph before you finished college, they would become a burden and she didn't want that."

Luke paused with the glass halfway to his mouth. That sounded so much like Ezzie. She wasn't the type to seek a handout or abuse her power. If he had known about his son, he would've been there for her in any way she needed. He groaned. Fuck, he had been an asshole to her all over again. And here he thought he'd grown out of it.

"What about after I graduated? Why didn't you tell me then?"

"By the time you graduated, I had decided it was no longer my place. Esmeralda was the one who needed to tell you. I could only nudge her in the right direction whenever I visited."

"While you were nudging her, did you bother to give her options on what to say?"

His mother had a way with words. It took her fifteen sentences to convey one idea. She had to make things more complex than they actually were; this was no different. One of them should have told him. Instead, his mother placed it all on his ex-girlfriend. Knocking the rest of the Jack Daniels back, Luke eyed the small row of mini-bottles on the refrigerator. A second one might be just what the doctor ordered.

Pursing her lips, his mother raised a sculpted eyebrow. "Has she told you Joseph's full name?"

"No. Why?"

Not that he'd bothered to ask either. He'd been focused on her case. Well, mostly focused. Okay, focused when it was necessary. His mind wandered onto a lot of things when the case wasn't forefront and center in his brain.

"You should ask her."

"Mom—"

His mother held her finger against her lips and shushed him. "Trust me on this. Put the empty glass down, brush your teeth, pull yourself together and go talk to her."

There was no point in arguing with his mother; she had spoken, which meant he pretty much had to do as he'd been told. He was twenty-seven years old and she still had that kind of effect on him. Getting to his feet, Luke set the glass down on a table. "Fine. I'll go talk to Ezzie."

Ezzie pressed the block of cheddar against the metal grater and shredded the cheese.

She'd been home a couple of hours now and hadn't heard a word from Luke. After he'd run out of the hotel room, she got to her feet and started after him. She didn't make it far. Instead of chasing him, she stood there and stared at the closed door. What kind of comfort could she offer him? All she had were apologies.

A sense of déjà vu filled her in that moment.

If she hadn't known better, she would've sworn they had gone back five years and switched places. It felt like they had returned to the beginning of their relationship and begun everything all over again.

Lifting the shredder, she dumped the pile of cheddar cheese into a bowl, and then moved onto the block of mozzarella. Ezzie glanced to her son. "Dinner will be ready soon. Go wash your hands."

"Okay, Mommy." Joey headed for the hallway.

There was a knock on the door.

Joey turned around toward the door.

Brushing her hands on her apron, she pointed in the direction of the bathroom. "Go. Now."

He giggled and darted down the hallway.

Stepping away from the kitchen, she opened the front door and blinked. Not only was her ex on her doorstep, but he'd completely discarded the suit. It had been quite some time since she'd seen him in jeans and a t-shirt. She didn't even know he still owned them. But dear god, he looked sexy as hell the way the denim gripped his lean and muscular legs. And the way the dark gray t-shirt adhered to his biceps. Fuck, she had to stop ogling him like this.

"Luke."

"Hey, Ez."

"What are you doing here? I'm sorry. That came out wrong."

Luke reached out for her, then after a second let his hand fall back to his side. "It's okay. I kind of deserve that. I shouldn't have gotten upset with—"

"Uncle Luke! You're here! Are you going to eat dinner with us?" Joey skidded to a stop beside Ezzie.

Her son had gone back to calling him uncle. Ezzie did her best to hide her cringe. It didn't bother her that Joey had used a term of endearment. It was just a reminder of the truth she'd been hiding and the decisions she had to make. Soon.

Getting on his haunches, Luke crouched down to her son's height. "Hey, buddy. You know, I'd love to stay for dinner, but I think that's up to your mom."

"Please, please, please! Oh please, Mommy!" Bouncing up and down, Joey laced his fingers together and pleaded.

Standing up, Luke shifted his gaze back to her. "Maybe we can talk after?"

She could easily refuse her son's request, but she owed Luke a conversation. Not just about the secret she'd offloaded earlier, but her inquiry too. "Yeah, he can join us."

"Yes!" Joey exclaimed, then high-fived Luke.

He grabbed Luke's hand and tugged him inside the door. "Come on!"

"Where are we going?"

"To wash our hands."

Ezzie raised an eyebrow and shut the front door. Didn't her son already wash his hands? She opened her mouth to say something, then decided against it as the two of them disappeared down the hall. Kind of seemed pointless. If he wanted to wash his hands again, she'd let him.

Meant he could share something with the father he didn't know.

That had to change; as soon as she could decide how to tell him.

Something was going on with Ezzie, but Luke couldn't complain. Wherever she had gone inside her head all throughout dinner had warranted him the blessing of being able to put his son to bed. Though he was still trying to muddle his way through what he presumed to be a simple task.

Luke fumbled a little as he tucked the covers around Joey for the third time. "I think we got it this time, bud."

Joey wiggled. "Not too snug, but just right. Will you tell me a story, Uncle Luke?"

Shit, that's right. Ezzie had done that last night, hadn't she? He had never been able to weave stories. He worked in facts. Even when he did share stories, it was an accumulation of factoids.

Luke frowned. "I don't really know any, but … maybe I can read you one."

"I'd like that."

"Do you have a favorite?"

His son waggled his finger for him to come closer and whispered. "Yes, but you can't tell Mommy. She doesn't know I have it."

"Have what?"

Sitting up, Joey reached over to his nightstand and opened the top drawer. He dug out a folded-up piece of paper and handed it to Luke. "My favorite story."

What kind of story was on a sheet of paper? He unfolded the paper to a letter. It wasn't addressed to anyone in particular' well it was, but not by name. It was definitely Ezzie's hand-writing and her signature at the bottom. "What's this?"

"It's to my daddy. Mommy did a whole bunch, but I like this one best."

His eyes widened? Ezzie had written him? She had told him that a few days ago, hadn't she? But he'd never received anything. How was that possible? Luke eyed the letter in his hand. What if she never mailed them? But then why would she have claimed to have sent them?

"Are you going to read it?" Joey asked.

"Umm, yeah. Of course."

Giving the letter a final once over, Luke cleared his throat and read the letter out loud.

"My dearest love,

You'd be so proud of your son today. We were down at the pool and he decided he was too big to be swimming with floaties. I tried to convince to be a bit more patient, but he argued with me until he got his way. I swear if I hadn't known any better, I would've believed I was speaking to you. He ticked off every reason on his hand as if there was no other way. Off the floaties went. And what did he do once they were gone? He jumped into the pool and made a big splash. At first, I laughed, until I realized he didn't come back up. I hopped to my feet and dove in to grab him, but couldn't find him anywhere. I came back up for air to see him sitting on the side of the pool, lounging like it was nobody's business. After making sure he was okay, I asked him what happened. His words to me were, "I held my breath." No other explanations, just that. I figured out what he meant later at dinner. Apparently, your son has been practicing holding his breath underwater at bath time, so that when he was finally free of his floaties he could scare the living crap out of me. I swear, he's more like you every day. I wish you could see it.

Forever yours,
  Ezzie"

He turned back to his son, who was already fast asleep. Brushing some of Joey's brown hair to the side, Luke kissed his forehead and carefully extracted himself from the bed. He tiptoed around the bed and returned the letter to the drawer his son had removed it from.

Lingering by the nightstand, he watched the rise and fall of his son's chest. In her letter, Ezzie made it sound as if their son was a miniature version of him. In a small way, he could see that. They shared so much in facial features, but it went beyond that to personality. Given how much he'd already missed, it was hard to agree with her stance. Yet the letter … God, that letter. His son had said she'd written a whole bunch.

What did that mean?

Were they talking about a small stack? Like four or five over the years? Or something that could reach closer to a hundred or more? Luke glanced toward the bedroom door.

One way to find out.

With a towel in her hand, Ezzie dried the last of the dishes and placed the plate in its proper cabinet. It had been an interesting turn of events for the night. Her normal bed time routine had been placed in Luke's hands. She had listened by her son's bedroom door for a few minutes before returning to the kitchen. The interaction between Luke and their son had been the sweetest thing she'd heard in a long time.

She hoped they could maintain that if she wound up in jail.

The hairs on the nape of her neck stood at attention. She didn't have to look for the cause. The way his presence affected her hadn't changed over the years. She didn't know if that was a good or bad thing.

"He's asleep."

"Good." Ezzie turned around and hung the dish towel on the handle of the oven.

Luke leaned against the kitchen counter and draped one ankle over the other. "Did you really write that letter?"

Lowering her gaze, she propped her hands up on the stove. Of course, she should've known her son would show him that. It was amongst hundreds of letters she'd penned. Most of which had gone un-mailed as several had been returned *"Return to sender."* She'd verified the address with her brother, then concluded Luke didn't want to be bothered. "Yes, I did."

"How many?"

Too many for her to count, but he couldn't really be asking for that. Could he? Letting go of the stove, Ezzie shifted her gaze to him. Even with his eyes narrowed, broad shoulders tightened and his face scrunched up he looked gorgeous. Yet it all told her how much he desired an answer from her.

An idea popped into her head. It wasn't a great idea. Hell, it wasn't even a good one, but what other choice did she have? They'd fought over this once before. But maybe if he saw it for himself, she'd get him to see the truth.

"Come with me."

She walked past him, strode down the hallway and headed straight for her bedroom at the back of the apartment. Opening her bedroom door, Ezzie gestured for him to sit on the bed. She ducked over to her closet and pulled down three small, light brown boxes. Stacking them together, she set them on top of the floral comforter atop her bed.

"I can't give you an exact number, but there's probably close to three hundred in there. Maybe more. I wrote at least one a week over the last five years, though sometimes I wrote more, especially during the last trimester of my pregnancy."

Luke regarded the stack of boxes in front of him. He swallowed to wet his parched throat. How was he supposed to react to this? Ezzie had just slammed three boxes of proof in front of him as to how many times she had attempted to contact him. And he didn't get a single one of them.

Steadying his shaky hand, he lifted the top off the first box. His eyes widened. It was exploding with folded letters like the one his son had requested he read. "None of these are in envelopes."

"Only the bottom box has those. I stopped sending them after they started coming back."

"What are you talking about?"

"See for yourself."

He moved the first two boxes and got into the bottom box. Sure enough, several of the letters were neatly tucked inside envelopes. Luke removed one of the envelopes. It had clearly been addressed to him and nothing appeared wrong with the address, but in big, fat, red letters *Return to sender"* had been scrawled.

He shook his head. "I didn't get any of these."

All of these letters and not a single phone call. She could've done so much more to give him a chance to be involved. Luke shoved the letters back in the box. "Why didn't you call when they started coming back? I would've been there."

Ezzie glared at him. "I did call. I called before I bothered to tell Nate, before I even started sending the letters. They were a last resort. And the one time I did call, another woman answered the phone. So, don't you dare try spinning this back on me."

"What woman? There hasn't been any other woman since you."

Shit. He hadn't meant to admit that. Despite its truth, the last thing his ex-girlfriend needed to know was that he hadn't dated another woman since they split up. If that's what you could even call it. It wasn't exactly like they spoke at all after their last fight.

"I presumed the blonde you cheated on me with, but I can't say for sure because I didn't bother asking for her name. I didn't really care to know." She crossed her arms.

She hadn't ever heard him out on what had happened back then. This time he wasn't going to give her a choice. With a growl, Luke leapt to his feet. "I didn't cheat on you! Jessica kissed me!"

"Shh, keep your voice down. I don't want Joey to wake up." Ezzie went to the bedroom door. She paused for a second, and then shut it.

Luke inhaled deeply and exhaled slowly. He didn't mean to get loud. Waking their son was the last thing on his mind. That would cause a conversation that was better left for another day. But he had to get her to hear him out. On to round two. Or was it round three?

"I didn't kiss her. I pushed her away. You just happened to arrive right when she kissed me."

"It shouldn't have mattered what time I got there. Or who kissed who. You put yourself in that position, which shouldn't have happened in the first place."

He opened his mouth to object, but he couldn't. His apology to Jessica had been necessary. It relieved the weight on his shoulders and allowed him to let go of the past. That was where it should've ended, instead of him hugging Jessica and opening himself up to a whirlwind of pain. How did he explain that Ezzie?

Just tell her the truth, asshole. All of it. His subconscious should really shut up. Luke gripped the nape of his neck. "You're right. I'm sorry for that. I knew Jessica being there was a coincidence, but I shouldn't have let her get that close to me. I guess … I thought it was a chance to close one door when I was trying to open another."

"Meaning what?"

Everything. The day should have changed their entire future. If he had caught up with her … if she hadn't seen the kiss … if the kiss had never even happened … they would've been raising their son together. They might have gotten married in the last couple of years. Or maybe working on baby number two. Luke smiled. Could they still have all of that?

Maybe, but he'd have to lay it all out on the line. "You know how you used to tell me I was self-deprecating and you thought it was because of a girl? Well, it wasn't a girl who hurt me. I was the one who hurt someone and that guilt stayed with me."

"So, what you're saying is the person you hurt was Jessica? And you talked to her to assuage that guilt. What I don't understand is what any of that has do with the kiss."

Luke dropped his hands to his hips. Shit. She had a valid point. Nothing he said explained it. He replayed that afternoon in his head. "Just before I left for college, Jessica told me she was pregnant. I panicked. I handed her cash, told her to take care of it and I left. Shortly after that, she miscarried. She tried calling me, but I never answered. That was the first time I'd seen her since then."

Ezzie stared at him for the longest time without saying a word. Tears welled in the corners of her eyes, and she glanced at the boxes of letters sitting on the bed. "You never answered."

Oh god! Not for one second had he considered what she would take away from that. Shit! Luke grabbed her arm, which she quickly yanked from his hold.

"It's not the same thing. I swear to God; I didn't receive a single letter.

And I never saw a phone call. If I'd seen you call or even an unknown number, I would've answered regardless of what I was doing or who I was with. I was ready to tell Nate about us. That's why, even after he told me you were pregnant, I came here. I didn't—"

"What? When?" She wiped at her face.

"Umm, I think you were about six months along … give or take a month. I couldn't see much. Your roommate kind of prevented me from coming in."

There were no outside windows by the front door. He'd gotten about a five second glimpse when the door had first cracked open and it had only been her and some guy in the kitchen. He hadn't been able to make out much else at the time. As much he hadn't wanted to believe she was carrying another man's child, it had been a slap in the face that told him otherwise.

"That doesn't … no … Matt would never do that."

"I promise he did. Ez … you weren't the only one that reached out. I did too. I called every chance I got, but I only ever got your voicemail. Every single time I left a message begging you to call me back, but I didn't know your number had changed. I apologized to Jessica when I saw her because I was ready for us to have a future together. I was ready to tell your family about us. I would've faced any consequence head on. I didn't care what happened, as long as I had you."

He peered into those sapphire blue eyes of hers. He didn't know if she believed him, but he hoped she did. The last few days had reminded him of everything they had. And if they could make their way through all the crap that had built up over the years, maybe, just maybe they had a shot of making their relationship work.

She swallowed. "What are you saying?"

That was a good question; one he absolutely knew how to answer. Closing the distance between them, Luke tucked a loose strand of her mahogany hair behind her ear. He caressed her cheek and fused his lips to hers.

Ezzie nipped his bottom lip and stroked his tongue with hers, then their tongues entangled together.

Fuck, he had missed her, but he didn't want to push things too far. Releasing the kiss, Luke dropped his forehead to hers and the answer to her question left his mouth before he had a chance to stop the words.

"Ez, I was in love with you. I'm still in love with you."

six

EZZIE KEPT REWINDING THE NIGHT before in her head. Never mind the kiss. That didn't bother her, although it should; she kind of liked it. But everything else that had been said about her best friend … it couldn't be true. That wasn't even half of what had been on repeat in her brain over the last several hours. Shoving her hands in the warm, soapy water, she rewashed the bowl she had already cleaned two times.

She had only half acknowledged Luke's proclamation of love. Nothing had come out of her mouth when those words had slipped past his lips. She had no clue how to reply. Back before their relationship had gone to shit, she'd been completely in love with him. Her feelings hadn't changed even in the months following their split. It had been the reason she'd started writing him letters in the first place. The failed call hadn't been enough to dissuade her their relationship couldn't work.

If nothing else, they could be amicable for their son's sake.

Luke understood that, didn't he?

Absolutely. He'd been so gracious about her inability to respond.

"That's okay. You don't have to say anything," Luke said.

She stared at him, slack-jawed. The butterflies in her stomach settled. Her heart thudded inside her chest. How many times had she imagined him saying those exact words? How many nights had she woken up to discover it had all been a dream? Ezzie blinked. She had to say something, but what?

"The letter Joey had me read ... how old was he?"

Déjà vu slapped her in the face once again. Except this time, she wasn't the one deflecting; he was. The last time this had happened ... it was the first time he'd asked about her butterfly tattoo. He'd allowed her to change the subject back then. Now, it was her turn to return the favor.

Ezzie cleared her throat. "He uh, it was um, six months ago. Just before his fourth birthday."

"Done, Mommy."

Snapping back to the present, she looked to her son and watched as he put his empty breakfast bowl on the counter. Loosening her grip on the bowl in the kitchen sink, she collected the dish and dropped it into the water. "Okay. Go brush your teeth."

She really had to stop thinking about last night. No, she couldn't. She had to find out if what he'd said about Matt was true.

It just didn't make any sense. Matt had always known how she felt about Luke. She had told him one teary-eyed night after they'd moved to California. Shit. Had that been the night she tried calling Luke and some woman had answered? It could have been.

But it didn't make sense that Luke would lie either. Nothing would cause a rift between them more than a lie, especially when it came to her best friend.

There was only one way to resolve this. She'd point blank ask Matt when he came by that morning to pick up her son. It would be one problem down and ... how many more to resolve? Ezzie groaned.

She couldn't even think about what Luke was awakening inside of her. Maybe she hadn't buried her feelings as deep down as she thought. Or maybe they had been sitting there this whole time.

Waiting.

Shit. Why had she never thought about that? Why had she always assumed they'd only ever have their past and their son?

The idea her and Luke could have a future had disappeared. Hadn't it? She had gone on a few dates after her son was born, but nothing since. And she most certainly hadn't slept with anyone since Luke. Chewing on the inside of her cheek, she finished cleaning the last two bowls in the water, rinsed them and placed them in the dishwasher rack to dry.

Should she really be entertaining the possibility of a reconciliation? Her trial was due to start next week and they hadn't found enough evidence to discredit the charges yet. But oh, how he made her feel. He hadn't been in the house in over eight hours and his presence still lingered. Ezzie bit her bottom lip. Her heels clicked against the tile as she crossed to the other side of the kitchen. With a smile on her face, she snagged a mug from the cupboard.

"Hello, hello."

Scooping up the newspaper on the doormat, Matt let himself into Ezzie's place. He didn't mind taking his godson to pre-school. The kid talked … a lot, which he took full advantage of. He had to determine how much time Luke spent around the apartment. Every second increased the chance Ezzie would find out what he'd done. He absolutely, one-hundred percent did not want her to find out about his involvement in keeping her and Luke apart.

"Good morning." She sipped from her coffee mug.

He squinted his eyes. That wasn't any old mug in her hands. It was her favorite mug. The one she only ever got out when she had a good night. He hadn't seen her use it in forever.

Closing the door behind himself, Matt sauntered into the kitchen. "Has there been a break in your case?"

"Sort of. We found contracts for investors I've never used, but we still need more."

"Then what has sparked this glint in your eye, pray tell?"

It sure as hell couldn't have anything to do with the paperwork she'd just mentioned. That left one other option. *Please, let me be wrong*, he thought. It wasn't that he didn't like Luke; he just didn't trust the guy. Even when he had shown up at their door a few years back, everything that had come out of his mouth had all been about what he needed, what he wanted. Not once had anything been said about what might be good for Ezzie.

Which was exactly why he'd sent the guy packing and then when she asked who had been at the door, he told her Jehovah's Witnesses. The fun part had been figuring out how to explain them getting past the doorman downstairs. Matt rolled his eyes. Good thing he'd always been quick on his feet.

"I just had a good night."

Taking a mug from one of the cabinets, Matt poured himself some coffee and added in about four spoons full of sugar. He handed Ezzie her newspaper. "You're being very vague."

"I'd say you're being very nosey, but it's no more than usual."

Clawing at the air, he hissed. "Retract the cat claws. There's no need for them. If you want to keep your exploits to yourself, by all means, do so. Who am I to judge?"

It wasn't like he told her everything that went on between him and Colin. She had an imagination. Though she probably didn't want to imagine two guys going at it like wild bucks. At least not any more than he longed to picture two women having it out or even a woman and man loving on one another. Ulch. Matt shuddered at the thought.

"There was no exploit. Luke and I just talked. That's all."

He would've believed that was all that had gone on if it hadn't been for the rouge in her cheeks. Those big ass devils told him she was lying. Maybe not entirely, but she certainly hadn't delivered the whole truth. "If you say so, Pinocchio."

"We did do a lot of talking. I showed him the letters and he told me he had come out here ... to California."

"Oh?" Matt swallowed. He couldn't let her see him sweat. So what if he'd lied? So what if he'd showed Luke the door? So, what if he'd hidden her phone? So what if he'd deleted the guy's voicemails? Everything he'd done had been to protect her.

"Yep. He had some rather interesting things to say about it."

"Like what?" *Brush it off,* Matt told himself. He had to act as if he had no clue what she was referring to. He refused to openly admit to what he'd done. She'd never forgive him.

"Like how the two of you talked at the front door. And that you'd told him I'd moved on."

Shit. Shit, shit, shit! How the hell was he supposed to defend that? He couldn't very well continue pretending like he was utterly clueless. Well, he could, but she'd see right through it. Becoming a mother had put some kind of sixth sense in her eyes. She'd been pregnant back then, which had been his only saving grace. That, and her distraction with Colin in the kitchen that day. He had to explain this somehow. Matt opened his mouth to say something—

"Teeth brushed, Mommy."

Matt exhaled a sigh of relief. His godson's interruption had never been more welcomed.

Ezzie narrowed her eyes at Matt, but only for a second before she turned her attention to her son. "Top and bottom?"

"I did both. You want to smell?" Joey paused in front of her and breathed in her face.

"Minty fresh. Come on; let's get your backpack so your Uncle Matt can get you to school." Ezzie ruffled his hair. Setting her mug aside, she started for the front door and opened the newspaper.

Matt shook his head and followed after them, then almost bumped into Joey who practically crashed into his mother.

She had stopped without a word. Her eyes glued to the newspaper in her hands.

He glanced over her shoulders, but all he caught was the headline: *Local Baker Hooks Up in Multiple Ways.* What the hell?

"Let's go, now. Come on, we need to go." Ezzie ushered them out the door like the building was on fire.

Ezzie banged on the door to Luke's hotel suite for the second time. Where was he? Why hadn't he answered yet? Fuck. This wasn't good. Not good at all. She glanced at the front page of the newspaper in her hand. "Damn it," she mumbled.

Fuck. He needed to—

The door swung open wide. Luke stood there with a crisp, light-blue shirt half unbuttoned. The two sides created a nice vector revealing part of the light brown hair on his sculpted chest.

"Ez? What are you doing here?"

Leering at the six-pack playing peek-a-boo, she bit the inside of her bottom lip. What had she come there for again? Her grip tightened around the newspaper in her hand. Oh! Right. She pushed her way inside and shoved the newspaper against his body. Her fingers grazed his chest. Ezzie swallowed.

Goosebumps crawled up her arms. Crikey, he felt so good. Nope. Nope. She couldn't think about that. Not now. She had to gain control of herself. Clearing her throat, she pointed to the newspaper. "Take a look."

With a sigh, Luke closed the door and unfolded the newspaper. His eyes scrunched as he looked from the paper then back to her. "Okay. And?"

And? That was all he had to say? The photograph showed him holding her in front of the courthouse. The headline was bad enough. It made it sound like she hadn't just ripped her so-called investors off, but that she was sleeping with her defense attorney. And all of that was before anyone even read the article.

"Are you not seeing how damaging this is?"

"How is it damaging? It has no impact on what we can prove in court."

"But this impacts my reputation. With my customers, my vendors and anyone we might get on a jury. Luke, the article makes me sound like a con-woman trying to sleep my way out of this mess."

It vilified her in the worst way. Nothing in the article had been false, although she wished it had. Then she'd have a reason to force the paper into a retraction. Instead, it talked about her arrest at the bakery, what she had been accused of, and then tacked on information about her relationship with Luke. Okay, so that wasn't currently true, but she didn't think that gave her grounds for a retraction.

Luke grabbed her shoulders and squeezed. "One, I have no intention of letting this get to a jury. They're too unpredictable. Two, even *if* we were sleeping together, it would have no influence on your case or how I defended you. Three, once we prove your innocence, that is what your customers and vendors are going to remember. Trust me on this."

She had no argument for his first two reasons, but his third ... she wasn't so sure about that. Her customers ranged anywhere from college students needing a sugar rush to older locals in search of a good bakery. Most of the locals had become regulars. And this was something they'd never forget. The accusation and arrest alone had created immutable damage to her character, but calling her out as a slut only cemented her as a criminal in search of her next target.

That's all she'd be remembered for. No one would talk about her devil's chocolate cupcakes, or her cherry Chocolate-chip cupcakes, or her pineapple strawberry upside-down cake. Nothing would be said about her frosted berry cake, or her vanilla wafer muffins. All that would be in people's memories were the charges she faced and that she used her sex-appeal to resolve the situation. Tears prickled at the corners of her eyes.

"You don't know my regulars. College students change all the time, but the older folks who frequent my bakery ... this will completely alter their opinion of me. And it'll ruin my credibility with my vendors."

He set the paper aside. Using his thumb, he swept the tears from her face. Luke brushed a tender kiss to her forehead and cradled her in his arms. "Listen to me. I know this seems pretty bleak, but I promise it isn't. We'll find out the truth, and then get the paper to print a new story. Your vendors, your customers, they will see that whoever caused all of this is the real criminal. Not you. I swear to you; this is not the end of your career or your bakery. Have a little faith."

Pressing her ear against his broad chest, Ezzie focused on the sound of his heartbeat. She didn't have a lot of faith these days. Everything she thought she knew about their time apart was false. The people she counted on the most had disappeared or betrayed her. Though ... that wasn't entirely true. Was it?

Luke had volunteered to take on her case. And he had kept her in the loop on every step, even their last trip to the courthouse. As for their personal life ... he'd opened up. Not just about their past, but that there was still something there. He hadn't offered a single reason for her not to trust him. That was enough.

"I have faith in you."

A smile crossed his face. The situation with the news story didn't thrill him, but he absolutely loved the fact that of all the people Ezzie believed in, he was one of them. He planned to do everything in his power to keep that faith.

Loosening his hold of her, Luke cupped her chin. "You know I'd do anything to protect you, right?"

"I know. I just ... I don't know. I'm worried."

Aside from him doing his job, there wasn't any reason for her to not be concerned. There was a lot at stake. Not just for her, but him too. He could care less about how losing her case affected his career. His only priority was how it affected them and their family. Yes, she had suggested he be prepared to take care of their son if she wound up in jail, but he preferred that never come to pass.

Luke caressed her cheek. "I know you are, but I promise I'll do everything I can to keep you safe. I lost you once. I'll be damned if I lose you again."

Ezzie bit her bottom lip. Their eyes locked. Her lips crashed against his.

Wrapping his arm tightly around her waist, he pulled her close. He penetrated her mouth with his tongue. Desire coursed through his veins. An uncontrollable need had been building since that first kiss the day before. The second kiss hadn't helped and hadn't gone far enough. Luke fisted a handful of her silky hair and deepened the kiss.

She moaned into his mouth.

Fuck! He'd forgotten how addictive that sound was. Then there was her taste. She still tasted like strawberries, his favorite fruit in the world. Entangling his tongue with hers, he fused their lips together.

Her hand balled up the back of his shirt, tugging at the buttons.

Shit. If she yanked a little bit more, he'd lose the shirt all together. His body cried out for him to let go already. *Drop the shirt and take this where you know you want to go.* But he couldn't. Not yet. Curling his hand at the small of her back, Luke released the kiss. His heart pounded beneath his chest as ragged breaths left his mouth.

Breathing heavily, her glassy eyes lifted to his. "I'm sorry."

As much as he longed to be inside of her, they had to focus on finding this accountant of hers. The list of things they had to accomplish for the day was fairly long and their time got shorter and shorter by the minute.

Luke nuzzled her nose. "Don't apologize. Believe me, I want you. But I want to figure out your books more. Getting you out of this mess is my top priority."

"Now I feel like I need to apologize for delaying our progress." Ezzie grinned and untangled herself from his arms.

Still the same smartass he remembered. He shook his head and straightened his shirt. Tucking the shirt into his pants, he crossed the room, picked up the red and blue striped tie he'd laid out on the bed and stopped. He hadn't paid much attention to the tie he'd selected for the day.

It was one Ezzie had picked out for him. Slipping it around his neck, he glanced at her and recalled what she'd told him. *These colors suit you well. They represent the hero you'll one day be to people.*

He didn't give a whole lot of thought back then to what she'd said, but now ... she had described him to their son the same way. Which reminded him, he'd never asked about their son's name as his mother recommended. "I meant to ask you. What name did you give our son? I've only ever heard you refer to him as Joey or Joseph."

Ezzie had already turned around to face him. She inhaled and exhaled deeply. "Joseph Lucas."

"You named him after me?" He and his son didn't share the same first name, but his name was a part of his son. He hadn't expected that.

"Yes. I wanted him to carry a part of you with him, always."

"When was the last time you actually spoke to your accountant?"

That was a good question. She had to think. Ezzie exited the off-ramp from the highway and turned right. She'd been arrested a week ago. Her bail had been posted the next day, which meant her last conversation had to have been last Monday. That's right she'd gone by his office because she'd noticed a discrepancy in the books.

Ezzie stopped her Jeep at a red light. How could she have forgotten about that? It had been an account she had never seen before. When she'd asked Jonathan about it, he told her he'd look into it. But then he'd never called and she had gotten arrested two days later.

"Holy shit."

"What?"

A horn blared behind her. She blinked. The light had turned green. Shaking her head, Ezzie shifted her foot to the gas pedal and drove forward. "Monday afternoon I checked over the books and I noticed there had been some transfers to an account I had no knowledge of, so I swung by Jonathan's office and questioned him about it. That was the last time we spoke. With everything going on, it completely slipped my mind."

"Do you remember anything about the account? Transfer dates? Amounts?"

"That's the thing; there was no discernible pattern, which is what made it stand out. I know all of my vendors. I've been using the same ones since I opened. I know what they cost. With this, the amount of money that was transferred was never the same and it didn't fall into any of my order timeframes."

She had only figured out two things that day. One: the amount of monies transferred out equated to thousands of dollars gone. Two: the account that received the funds had a blanket name on her books.

"This gives us something to search for. When we get back to my hotel room, we'll need to find the copies of your books in the evidence boxes. And your bank statements. We'll have to look for those too, but just to cover our bases, I'll subpoena records from your bank."

Ezzie turned right on the street that Jonathan lived on and slowed down. Several of his neighbors worked from home or didn't work at all. With no accessible driveways, most of them parked on the street. Made locating a parking spot a little more difficult. There was an empty place close by, but it meant a small walk. Both she and Luke had opted for appropriate foot attire for their clothes, but that didn't make it practical.

"Are you okay walking a couple of blocks?"

"I can handle it. Can you?" A wide grin crawled on his face.

"Why Mr. Jonnihan, if I didn't know any better, I'd swear you're mocking me."

"I might be, but you are the one in high heels."

"I'm quite capable of maneuvering a sidewalk, thank you very much." Ezzie smirked and parallel-parked her Jeep in the closest spot available.

Her accountant's house was still a couple of blocks away, but she'd rather be there than spend the next twenty minutes hunting down a closer place to park. She shut off the ignition and climbed out of the vehicle.

She walked around the front of the jeep and approached the passenger side as Luke shut the car door.

Boom!

The ground beneath them shook and knocked her and Luke into the car. His arms shot around her and he quickly steadied them both. "Are you okay?"

"Yeah." Ezzie nodded. Freeing herself, she faced the direction of the noise.

Smoke plumed not too far off in the distance. She could clearly see fire reaching for the sky. She couldn't say for sure from where they stood which house had been engulfed in flames, but it looked like it was down near the cul-de-sac. "Oh, please!"

Please, don't let that be his house, she thought.

"What? Can you see the house?"

There was no time to answer him. Darting to the back of her Jeep, Ezzie yanked her heels off and shoved her feet in the sneakers she always kept in the trunk. She ran in the direction of the fire.

He didn't know what the hell just happened, but whatever it was had made Ezzie frantic. When she took off down the sidewalk, he followed after her. Luke stayed hot on her heels. It didn't take them long to cover a block and a half, but that was as far as they could get.

Ezzie skidded to a stop. Her eyes widened. "Oh God!"

The house had exploded. Bright orange flames licked at what remained of a pretty yellow house. At least he assumed it had been yellow. It was the only color he could make out from the rubble in front of the fire.

Car alarms screamed angrily. A couple of empty vehicles had been flipped onto their side. Several windows had been shattered. Debris scattered all over the street and into a few of the neighbor's yards. Whatever had caused the destruction to the house had been big.

Without another word, Ezzie started for the house.

Luke snagged her elbow. Going into that mess wasn't safe. They were about as close as they could get without putting themselves in harm's way. "What are you doing?"

"He could be in there!"

"Who?" Not that he imagined anyone survived that. The house was in complete shambles. If the explosion hadn't killed anyone inside, then the fire had. He just hoped the house belonged to anyone, but the one person they had been there to see.

"Jonathan Burke ... my accountant."

Fuck. Why, oh why, did he know that was the name she was going to utter? Luke glanced across the street. A few neighbors had come out of their homes. They'd probably felt the same movement he and Ezzie had a block away. This was bad. Very bad.

"Ez, if he was in there, nothing can be done to save him."

"So that means we don't even try?"

"Not when it puts either of us at risk. Right now, even the smallest well-intended action can do that. What we need to do is leave." His arm still hooked in hers, he nodded toward the gathering crowd.

Following his line of sight, Ezzie frowned. "Great."

"Let's just head back to the car. If we're lucky, they'll think we were doing exactly what they did; looking to see what happened."

Luke draped an arm around her shoulders and they walked together back to the car. It wouldn't take more than her presence and whatever destroyed the house to be determined wrongful for police to come knocking on her door. Something he was trying to prevent.

"I hope so."

"Me too, Ez. Me too."

He pressed a loving kiss to her forehead. Actually, he hoped they didn't get noticed at all, but he didn't expect a miracle.

Ezzie stabbed at the plate of spaghetti sitting on the table in front of her. She and Luke hadn't accomplished much once they'd returned to the hotel. The hours had gone by with the explosion continuously tap dancing on her brain. She hadn't been much use at all. So, she'd gone home, baked and watched the news for any reports on survivors.

The six o'clock news had covered the story. According to the reporter, no bodies had been found and no one had been injured. Only nearby vehicles and the house itself had received any kind of damage. The house had pretty much been demolished.

Several of the neighbors described it to the reporter as a loud boom followed by what felt like an earthquake. Kind of the same thing she and Luke had experienced. The anchor woman had gone on to say that early reports indicated a gas leak had caused the explosion.

"… and then he went *bam!*" Joey slammed his hand down on the table.

Shit! Ezzie jumped.

"Mommy, are you okay?"

"Yeah, honey. Your story startled Mommy, that's all." She plastered a smile to her face. Her son shouldn't be concerned with her inability to focus on him, something she really should be doing. Hell, she should be acting grateful she and Luke hadn't been closer to the house when the explosion had occurred.

Joey shrugged and looked back to Matt. "That's when I catched the ball."

"Well, I'm so glad you caught the ball and didn't get hit with the bat." Grinning, Matt glanced from her son to her and back again.

Was there something wrong with his eyes? Why was he looking at her like that? Was he trying to tell her something? Wait. What had he said? Something about a bat and a ball. The story her son had been sharing. Fuck. She really had to stop thinking about that … whatever it was … blast. It had happened, but no one had been hurt. That was the bottom line.

No, it wasn't. She hadn't spoken to Jonathan in over a week. All of her calls to him went to voicemail. His office space had been completely emptied and his house had blown up. The guy was nowhere to be found and everything related to him had been eradicated.

"Ezzie!"

Snapping out of her own head, she eyeballed Matt. She had zoned out again. Had her son recounted another story? God, she missed the days when everything was simple. "What?"

"Your son's trying to get your attention."

She gathered that much. Couldn't he have just subtly referenced what her son had said? No, he had to be obvious with her distraction. Ezzie turned toward her son. "I'm sorry, baby. What is it?"

"I'm full. Can I go watch T.V.?"

"Sure, sweetie."

Her son hopped out of his chair and headed directly for the living room.

She glanced at her half-eaten plate of spaghetti. Didn't look like much of a reason to pretend she was hungry. Ezzie got out of her chair and collected hers and her son's plate off the table.

Matt stood and trailed her into the kitchen. "What is going on with you? You have been spacing out all night long."

"I have a lot on my mind right now."

"I kind of figured that. What I'd like to know is what is so important you practically ignore your son?" Lowering his voice, Matt propped a hand on his hip and glared at her.

Where to start on that one? Let's see … her accountant had disappeared and could very well be one who framed her. Her ex-boyfriend was stirring emotions deep inside her soul that she had thought gone. Not to mention, he had also accused her best friend of lying to her. Ezzie crossed her arms and narrowed her eyes at Matt. Come to think of it, she had asked him about it that morning and he had brushed it off as if it was nothing.

Huh. She opened her mouth—

Her cell phone rang. Saved by the bell … again. She removed her phone from the pocket of her slacks and pressed it to her ear. "Hello?"

"Ez, I've got something. You need to come see this."

"Now?"

Luke had to be joking. Yeah, he had decided to hang back at the hotel and keep searching through all the documentation collected on her bakery. But did she really have to head back tonight?

Matt cocked an eyebrow at her.

"Yes. You're not going to want to wait," Luke said.

She sighed. This was going to be a long night. She could see it clear as the full moon shining through her balcony. "Okay. Um, give me thirty minutes."

"All right. I'll see you then." The line disconnected.

"What was that all about?"

Tucking her cell phone back in her pocket, she pinched the bridge of her nose. A trip to his hotel wasn't the best of decisions, but he sounded way too excited for it to be something small. Whatever it was, it had to be worth the trip out tonight.

"Luke said he found something. Think you could watch Joey for a bit?"

"I suppose so."

"Don't sound so enthusiastic about it."

"If he's really found something, then I'm happy for you. I just don't see why it can't wait until tomorrow."

What was with the attitude? He seemed … annoyed? Like in a matter of days she had become an inconvenience to him. Ezzie crossed her arms and frowned. "I don't know. He didn't say, but I'm not in any kind of position to argue with him. We only have a few days before my next court date and I'd really like to have this figured out before then. Is that okay?"

Dropping his hands to his hips, Matt narrowed his eyes at her. "Are you on your period? Because you're being awful crabby tonight."

"Oh, dear god." Of all the things for him to say. Not that she should be surprised any more. They'd known one another long enough to know which buttons to push. Ezzie rolled her eyes at his sarcasm and exited the kitchen.

"I mean, it would totally explain everything."

She waved off his comment. There was no need to dignify his asinine question with an answer. Stepping into the living room, she sat on the couch next to her son. "I need to head out for a couple of hours, so Uncle Matt is going to take care of you while I'm gone. Okay?"

"Can't Uncle Luke watch me?"

Ezzie blinked. Her son's question caught her completely off guard. She'd seen how easily he'd adapted to his father, but she hadn't been prepared for her son to want Luke around.

She swallowed. "Um, he can't tonight, baby, but I'll see if he can spend time with you tomorrow. Okay?"

"Okay, Mommy."

Giving him a quick hug and kiss, she got up, grabbed her car keys and purse and left.

seven

"WHAT EXACTLY AM I LOOKING at?"

"A video recording of one of the contract signings and it's not you."

Luke grinned. His private investigator had come through. Not only had Howard located digital proof that Ezzie hadn't been anywhere near any of the investment companies, she hadn't been the one to sign any of the contracts. Only one of the firms recorded their meeting, but they only needed one.

"I can see that, but that can't be why I had to come so late."

You could've told me all this over the phone, Luke thought.

She didn't say it, but it had been silently understood. He pointed to the brunette sitting at the conference table in the video. "I told you to come because I'm hoping you recognize this woman. Proving you had no involvement and being able to prove who's actually responsible are two different things. We have to keep digging if we're going to be able to do both."

She half-shrugged and took the tablet from his hands. Perching on the edge of the bed, Ezzie studied the video for several minutes. "Are there any other angles?"

"The only other footage they had is from the receptionist desk." Luke accessed an e-mail account on the tablet and brought up that recording.

Biting her bottom lip, she watched that video and replayed it a second and third time. Her eyes widened. "Holy shit. I know who this is!"

"Who?"

"Veronica O'Reilly. She was Jonathan's assistant."

He was impressed. Most assistants got overlooked. Ezzie hadn't just identified the woman, but she knew her by name. Though it seemed a little strange the guy would employ a woman who could pass for Ezzie. Unless … it had been intentional. It made sense if Jonathan and Veronica were working together. Either way, they had taken a step in the right direction.

Luke walked over to the mini-bar and selected a couple of bourbon mini-bottles. "This is really good. You know anything about her? Address? Age? Kids? Something that might help us locate her."

"I know she lived in an apartment building near the university, but I don't know exactly where. She was single. No kids, but I think she had a dog."

"Do you know what kind of dog?" He poured some bourbon in each glass. Setting the empty bottles aside, he picked up the glasses and crossed over to the bed. He eased down next to Ezzie and handed her one of the drinks.

"What's this for?"

"A toast. We've made our first big break-through."

It may not have been much, but if it was all the further they got, then they could at least get her off. Not that it was near enough. He didn't want to just prove her innocence; he wanted to prove she'd been set up. It'd be a bonus if the real criminals got arrested in the process.

She held her glass up and they clinked them together. Ezzie sipped the bourbon and eyed the chestnut brown liquid. "That's really good."

Closing his eyes, he let the bourbon sit on his tongue a second before swallowing. It was like a small flame going down the back of his throat. *Oh, so good.* "Back to my last question. Do you know what kind of dog she had?"

"No. I think it was small and brown, but I'm not certain."

"Well … it's not a lot, but it's something for my P.I. to go on."

"I'm sorry. I never really talked to her."

"But you know her name?" Luke blurted the question out without a second thought. He hadn't meant it to sound derogatory, but it likely came off that way. Receptionists most often were nameless and faceless blobs. The only one who ever knew an assistant's name was the person they were assisting. And sometimes even that wasn't true.

"She had a placard on her desk with her name on it. And before you say anything about the dog, I saw a picture once on her computer. As for where she lived … she popped into the bakery on more than one occasion and she mentioned it happened to be close to her apartment."

Luke stood and navigated his way to the desk in the living room. He collected his cell phone and shot a text off with all the information Ezzie had relayed about this Veronica O'Reilly. "You may not have befriended her, but you got some good intel that should narrow down the search grid for my P.I."

"I still can't believe you have a private investigator on your payroll." Getting to her feet, Ezzie set the tablet on the dresser and traipsed over to one of the evidence boxes.

"Yeah, well, he's come in handy." He knocked back the last of the bourbon in his glass and snaked two more of the mini-bottles. Holding one out, Luke joined her by the box she'd gone digging through.

"Care for another?"

Chewing the inside of her cheek, Ezzie regarded the tiny bottle of amber liquid Luke offered. If she was smart, she'd decline and head back home. She took a gander at him and the way his chocolate-brown eyes softened made her heart race. One more drink wouldn't hurt. She finished the bourbon in her glass and held it out for a refill.

"Yeah. And maybe while I'm here we can go back to tackling my financial books."

"Sounds good to me." Luke screwed the cap off one of the mini-bottles and poured it into her glass, then did the same thing with the other one for himself.

"I'm sorry I kind of left you hanging earlier." Her head hadn't been in the right frame for document scanning, which was pretty much all they'd done. The lines at one point had begun blurring together. That was without alcohol. She wasn't sure it would be any different now, but she felt better than she had before.

"It's okay. I get it. This afternoon … it was overwhelming."

"Not for you."

He had been so cool about it all. He'd prevented her from running into the fire and even noticed the spectators that had gathered. She'd only been able to think about the possibility of someone trapped under the house. Or what was left of it.

"I live in a courtroom where figurative bombs get dropped all the time. I had to learn how not to act surprised when they did."

People lied. She hated the reality of it, but that was the truth of the matter. As a lawyer, of course, he dealt with it *all* the time. Ezzie swallowed more of the warm liquid in her glass. "How do you trust people when you face so many liars?"

"People like you remind me there are more people out there leading an honest life than there are liars."

She thought about the people who came into her bakery regularly: the Royce's, Ben Woods, Sarah Dowdall … they were the nicest and most honest people she knew. They were her reminders. She was forgetting one though, wasn't she? Ezzie looked from the box full of documents to Luke. "You remind me too."

"I'm happy to hear that." He flashed a wide grin revealing his pearly white teeth.

It wasn't one of those bright, charming smiles that made women's panties drop. Well, okay, it was, but there was more to it. Behind it was a quiet regard. One that said how much he cared about others. And it made her insides melt. That had been the smile she'd fallen in love with.

Setting the empty glass down, Ezzie caressed his cheek. "I've missed this smile."

"I could say the same about yours." Luke pressed a tender kiss to the inside of her hand.

Her pulse quickened at the brief contact. It sent shivers down the back of her spine. She might have a bit of a buzz. But at the moment, she couldn't tell if it was due to the alcohol or the sensation of his lips against her skin.

He brushed a trail of kisses along the inside of her wrist to her forearm. Gently tugging the satin material of her blouse aside, he kissed her collarbone, and then continued the path to her neck.

Ezzie moaned. God, this felt so good. *He* felt so good. *This is wrong. He's your lawyer.* And her ex-boyfriend. And her son's father. Why should his title matter? She had been fighting her feelings … her attraction to him for days. Fuck, she didn't have the strength anymore.

Shit, he should really stop this. He should—

The sound that passed her lips convinced him to keep going. Luke fused his lips to hers. He fisted a handful of her mahogany, silky locks. God, she felt … right. *So* right.

Her arms wrapped around his neck and her tongue stroked his.

That sent a jolt of electricity through his body. His dick hardened behind the fly of his slacks. There was no stopping himself this time. He had to have her. He needed to be inside her. As much as his body strained with desire, he intended to take his time.

His fingertips skated down her back until they reached the bottom of her blouse. He peeled the hem of the blouse from inside her dress pants, and then rested his hand at the small of her back and groaned. It had been so long since he'd felt the warmth of her skin beneath his touch.

Deepening the kiss, Ezzie yanked his shirt from his slacks and undid each button. She inched his arms apart and slowly pushed the shirt from his shoulders. It landed on the floor.

She released the kiss. With a ragged breath, her glassy eyes raked over his bared chest. Her gaze landed on the circle of blue along his side. Biting her bottom lip, Ezzie caressed the bruise and placed a gentle kiss right above it.

Luke watched as she created a path back to the top.

First, she kissed him on his lower abdomen, then nuzzled his belly button and slowly licked straight up his six pack.

His eyes rolled back at the subtle tease that sparked all of his pleasure sensors.

Ezzie pressed one final kiss to his chin, then partially unbuttoned her blouse and lifted her arms in the air.

He slipped her blouse over her head and tossed it on the floor. Beneath it, she had on a white lace bra that barely covered anything. Her breasts were still perfect, though they might have been larger than he remembered. Tucking some of her hair behind her ear, Luke swallowed.

It was strange. He was more nervous now than he had been the first time they'd ever been together. Back then, he knew they both longed for one another. Everything inside him told him not to stop, but he had to be certain.

"Are you sure about this?"

"Not in the least, but I'm tired of fighting it. Aren't you?"

How did he answer that? He was tired. Tired of trying to escape the memories, their past, the thoughts of what could've been, what was … even what should be. But maybe that was the point. They could have tonight and see what tomorrow brought them.

His lips crashed against hers. Their tongues entangled together. He enveloped her in his arms and cupped her ass. Tightening his hold, he hoisted her up and her legs came around his backside.

Carrying her, Luke walked forward.

Ezzie moaned again. She hardly noticed the cold, plush comforter underneath her skin as she was lowered onto the bed. All she could feel was the heat coming from Luke as his body sunk into hers.

With her leg around his ass, she squeezed and grinded against him. They still had a lot of clothes between them. And they really had to go. Pulling him closer, she massaged the muscles from his tailbone to his shoulder blades.

Leaving her lips, he nuzzled her neck, then latched onto one of her breasts through the lace material. Luke sucked on a nipple, making it pucker. He slid a strap of the bra down and swirled his tongue around the other nipple.

Her back arched and she gasped. Digging her nails into his shoulders, she raked her nails down his back.

Luke growled. He reached down, unbuttoned and unzipped her pants. Gripping at her hip, he shoved the other cup of the bra away and nipped at her breast. He lifted her ass and jerked her pants down her legs.

She laid there in nothing but a pair of white lace panties and matching bra, both straps hanging off her shoulders. Ezzie bit her bottom lip and drank in the sight of him as he loosened his own slacks and let them fall to the floor.

Nothing about him had changed over the years, from his hard jawline to his broad shoulders to his ripped abs. That was a six-pack she enjoyed tasting. It cut into an exquisite 'V' shape that led to a bulge in his boxers she wouldn't mind wrapping her mouth around. His lean, muscular legs completed the package.

For at least one night, it was all hers.

He dropped to his knees and traced kisses back up her calf and inner thigh. Hooking his thumbs in the band of her panties, he eased them down her legs and threw them over his shoulder. Making his way back up her body, he sucked on the inside of her thigh and licked between her folds.

"Oh, god!" She bucked at the sensation of his tongue. Fuck, it wouldn't take her long to come if he kept that up.

Luke stroked her slit, then penetrated her with his fingers. Keeping his fingers inside her, he crawled on the bed and locked his mouth around one breast while kneading the other.

Balling the comforter in her hands, she moaned. *Fuck!* A current traversed from the top of her head to the tips of her toes. All of her synapses lit up at once. Everything he was doing burned her from the inside out. Between his fingers and his mouth, she wouldn't last much longer.

Euphoria consumed her. Ezzie bunched up the comforter and her legs opened further for him. Pressure built in her lower belly. Her inner walls contracted.

"Oh god!"

The sensation of Ezzie coming around his fingers was too much. He couldn't wait any longer. Removing his fingers, Luke wrenched his boxers off, nearly ripping them in half.

He slammed deep inside her core and almost came himself. *Fuck me.* She felt too perfect. Her folds were so tight around his dick.

Staying still, he brushed a kiss against her lips. He needed a second. If he—

Ezzie rocked her hips.

Shit. Just her movement alone geared him up. Luke found her rhythm and pistoned in and out of her. Fuck. He definitely wasn't going to last long.

Lacing their fingers together, he met her thrust for thrust and buried his face into her neck. He tried slowing down a bit, but her core clenched around him.

"Fuck, Ezzie!"

She squeezed his fingers. Her nails dug into his shoulder blades. "Oh god, Luke!"

The little bursts of pain combined with her orgasm sent him over the edge. Heat shot up his shaft and set off his own release.

It had been more powerful than anytime he remembered being with her before. It was like his body knew it was home.

His chest dropped against hers.

Both of them panted heavily.

Catching his breath, he brushed a kiss across her lips and laid his head next to hers.

Ezzie lazily stroked up and down his back with her fingers.

Luke closed his eyes. He may not ever feel this again. If he did nothing else, he would imprint this moment in his memories for the rest of his life. He really hoped he got to experience this and more.

God, help him.

Right then, he desired nothing more than to have a second chance.

Matt fluffed Joey's pillow and tucked the covers around him. He glanced at the books on the bookcase next to the nightstand. "What are we feeling tonight?"

"No story tonight."

His godson had always wanted a story read to him. At least when he was around. Whether it was that letter he favored, a random father story that only Ezzie could tell, or something off the bookshelf.

"Are you sure?"

He nodded. "I'm sure."

"You're not feeling sick, are you?" Matt pressed the back of his hand against his godson's forehead. He didn't appear sick and he didn't feel sick. Then again, if the kid was sick, it would be easily known. He was as dramatic as his mother when it came to not feeling well.

"No." Joey grinned. "I just don't want a story. I'm a big boy tonight."

"Oh, I see."

Now it all made sense. He was determined to prove he'd be okay for a night without his mother. Unlike the night she'd gotten arrested. Matt and Colin had taken Joey in for the night and his godson had almost had a panic attack. How was that even possible for a four-year-old? He still hadn't figured that out.

Turning out the bedside lamp, Matt stood and started for the bedroom door. "Okay. No story. Get some rest."

"Uncle Matt?"

"Yeah?" He stopped halfway across the room.

"Do you think Uncle Luke likes my mommy?"

Oh, how to answer that? Honestly, of course he did, but he couldn't say that. No, he didn't want to say that. He fully believed Luke was all wrong for Ezzie. Matt sighed. He shouldn't tell his godson that either. "Your mom's a great woman, so … yeah, he might."

"Well, I hope she doesn't like him back. My daddy's coming home soon and I want us all to be together."

"Why do you think your dad's coming home?"

"I just do. I feel it in my tummy."

Oh, hell. Great way to make him feel like a piece of shit. Matt was the one who had sent Luke away. But he could fix that, couldn't he? All he had to do was tell his godson the truth. Luke was his father.

Matt opened his mouth and snapped it shut. What the hell was wrong with him? It wasn't his place to tell Joey the truth. That fell to Ezzie and Luke. Shit. He had to get out of that room before he did something stupid. Said something he couldn't take back. But he had to say something. His godson wouldn't accept anything less.

That left him one option: affirmation. "I'm sure you're right. Now, go to sleep."

"Hey, Uncle Matt?"

"Yeah, Joe?" Maybe he should've pushed for the story more. Would've minimized this conversation.

"If my daddy doesn't come back, do you think Uncle Luke would be my new daddy?"

Bite your tongue. Don't do it! In that moment, he wanted to tell his godson so badly that his father had technically come back. Not that Luke had ever been there. *And whose fault is that?* His subconscious needed to get with the program here. No matter what he said, he wouldn't hurt his godson's feelings.

Matt nodded. "You're a great kid. He'd be a fool if he didn't want to be. Now, go to sleep."

"Night, Uncle Matt."

"Good night."

He scurried to the door and closed it most of the way behind himself. That wasn't something he wanted to face again. He'd be sure to tell Ezzie. She needed to get her shit together anyway and tell Joey the truth, or at least something close to it. His godson may only be four, but he understood way more than he let on.

Matt was sure of it.

Ezzie rolled over to her side and light flashed her in the face. What the hell? Where had the light come from? She'd turned out every light in the house except for the nightlight in her son's bedroom and the bathrooms. She rubbed her eyes and focused on the direction of the light.

There was a digital clock on a nightstand next to her. It read 1:30 A.M. Fuck! This wasn't her bed! Or even her apartment. She and Luke made love last night. She must've passed out after the last time. Gathering her bearings, she glanced over her shoulder.

One of Luke's hands rested on his belly and the other above his head. He looked so peaceful. His brown hair ruffled from the multiple times she'd run her fingers through it. His lips were swollen from all the kissing. And ... was that a hickey on his neck?

Crikey. Had she done that?

A loud snore came out of Luke. He batted at his chest and readjusted, but he didn't wake up.

Good. He was completely asleep; she could move without disturbing him. Ezzie slowly extracted herself from the bed, then tiptoed around the room trying to find her clothes. Her bra had landed on the floor by the dresser, as had her pants. That left her blouse and underwear. If she had to, she could forego her panties, but she had to find her—wait, that's right. It had been taken off by the evidence boxes.

Thankfully, she'd removed her heels by the door so she didn't have to hunt them down. She gathered the articles of clothing she'd been able to locate and redressed in the other room.

Pausing in the doorway to the bedroom, she took one last look at Luke. She hated to leave like this, but she hadn't meant to fall asleep in the first place. She had to get home to her son.

With a smile on her face, she collected her purse and shoes and snuck out of the hotel suite.

Matt bolted upright and the magazine he'd been reading fell on the floor. Fuck. What time was it? He blinked a few times before eyeballing the time on his Michael Kors watch. Was it seriously almost two in the morning?

She had to be back by now, but she would've woken him up. He stretched and climbed off the couch. Strolling down the hallway, he poked his head in Ezzie's bedroom. Empty. Matt frowned. Where the hell—

The front door opened.

You've got to be kidding me, he thought.

He strode back down the hallway toward the dining room and narrowed his eyes. She looked different. Why did she look different? He scrutinized her from head to toe. Her dark hair was unkempt like a bird's nest. Her cheeks were flushed. The buttons on her blouse were crooked. And she wasn't wearing any underwear.

Matt gasped. "You had sex!"

"Shh! Keep your voice down."

"Are you out of your flipping mind?" He glowered at her. He hadn't babysat his godson so she could hook up with her ex-boyfriend. Never mind the fact that her ex just so happened to be her lawyer too.

"I didn't mean for it to happen. It just did."

"What'd you do? Fall on his dick?" Matt smirked and rolled his eyes. She did not seriously give the lamest excuse possible. Nope. Nun-uh. He didn't hear that idiotic statement come out of her mouth. *Yes, you did.*

"Excuse me? What the hell is your problem?"

Oh, he had *so* many issues. Where did he start? Her shagging her ex. Her being gone for nearly six hours. Her son completely unaware of his relationship to Luke. Matt crossed his arms.

"My problem is that I stayed to watch Joey so you could deal with stuff regarding your case, not get one last hoorah."

"Not that it's any of your goddamn business, but we did work on my case. As for everything else, that doesn't really concern you."

"Doesn't concern me? This is the guy who broke your heart. The guy who cheated on you. The guy who didn't bother to call. The guy who dropped you like a bad habit. And who was the one who picked up the pieces? Because it sure as hell wasn't him."

In his heart, he knew he'd gone too far. But he hadn't been able to stop the words from coming out. He was so pissed at her. So what if his lie was exposed? He no longer cared. If his best friend paid enough attention to what he'd said, then they could at least finally address it.

Like adults.

Or pseudo-adults.

Ezzie slapped him. "Screw you. Luke may have hurt me, but he didn't cheat on me. And he did call and he did show up, but you did something to intervene like you always do. I don't know what the hell you did Matt, but I'm done. I'm over the jealous puppy act because if this is how you are as a friend, then I sure as hell don't need it."

His cheek tingled. Yeah, he'd definitely gone too far, but he didn't think she'd hit him. He also didn't think she'd throw him in the trash the way she had. Her words stung more than the blow to the face.

Nodding, Matt walked around her and paused at the front door. "That's fine, but do me a favor. Focus on growing a pair and telling your son who his father is. He thinks Luke is trying to ruin your family."

"What?" Ezzie spun on the ball of her foot just as the front door shut. She stared at it for a second. Should she chase after him? Or let him go? Damn it! Damn it! Damn it! She took one step forward and stopped.

Her soul was split in two. One part of her screamed to go after him. This was her best friend. Yeah, he'd gotten in the middle of her relationships before, but it had always been to protect her. The other part of her said to let him go. He'd done enough damage for a lifetime. And he needed to understand his part in everything before they could even consider resolving their problems.

"Mommy?"

She dragged a hand down her face to wipe away the anger and disappointment from her fight with Matt. Silently she inhaled and exhaled a deep breath and turned around. "Yeah, baby?"

"What was that noise?"

Shit. Her son had overheard their argument. Maybe he didn't hear the words. His door would've been closed most of the way. It wasn't much in the way of comfort, but it was all she had.

Ezzie hugged her son. "I'm sorry, baby. Your Uncle Matt and I were just discussing something. We didn't mean to wake you up."

"Okay."

"Come on; let's get you back to bed." She ushered her son back to his bedroom and got him tucked into bed. It didn't take much for him to pass back out. Ezzie placed a loving kiss on his forehead, then headed for the bedroom door and lingered.

He thinks Luke is trying to ruin your family. Hanging her head, she disappeared into her own bedroom. Matt was right about one thing. She and Luke did have to figure out a way to tell Joey the truth.

Quickly.

Stretching his arms out, Luke patted the empty space beside him. He cracked open an eye. He had fallen asleep with Ezzie. Right? He hadn't just dreamt it. No way. His body felt—energized. He felt more alive than he'd been in the last five years. They had absolutely passed out tangled in one another's arms.

Last time he'd woken up alone, she was making breakfast. Not that there was much of a kitchen in this hotel suite. It was barely usable. And definitely not for a chef like her. Maybe she'd gone to get breakfast instead.

Tossing the covers aside, he got out of bed and scoured the room for a note. There was nothing. Nothing hastily scribbled anywhere. Her clothes weren't there either. Everything was gone, except her panties. He found those on the floor at the end of the bed.

Had she slipped out in the middle of the night? Why would she have done that? Their son had been with a babysitter. It wasn't as if he was alone. Even if she had felt the need to go home, why wouldn't she have woken him up? He would've gone with her.

His cell phone rang.

Maybe that was her.

Luke trekked back into the bedroom and scooped up his phone. He blinked. Was he seeing that right? Yes, he was, but there were a number of explanations. None of which included his best friend calling him.

"Hello?"

"I was beginning to think you weren't going to answer."

All right, he was wrong, but he'd take it. Hopefully it was a sign that their friendship was on the mend. Nate had ignored him since their fist fight Saturday. He couldn't fault the guy. He deserved at least one punch for not talking to him about his and Ezzie's relationship.

"Of course I would. I've been trying to get a hold of you all week."

"Yeah. I'm not ready to discuss that. I just wanted to see how my sister's case was going."

Luke rubbed the top of his brow. It would've been nice if Nate was open to talking about Ezzie, especially with what transpired last night. He wasn't positive they were trying to patch things up, but that was kind of how it felt. He probably needed to tell Nate that before things escalated further.

"Right. Um, well, Howard sent me some footage he obtained yesterday proving that Ezzie didn't sign the contracts. We've managed to figure out it was her accountant's assistant that forged her signature."

"Is Howard going to keep digging?"

"Yeah. He's, uh, trying to find out information on the accountant and assistant. Plus, there was some kind of issue with Ezzie's PC, so I've got Jake working on that."

They should know something soon on that end. It had been shipped off, what, four days ago? Yeah. He'd sent that out Monday and it was Thursday.

"Good. Sounds like everything is under control."

For the most part. No need to mention the explosion yesterday. Or the emptied office of the accountant. Those were minor details.

"Nate, I promise you, I'm doing all I can to get your sister's charges dropped."

"I believe you."

That was music to his ears. It meant a lot Nate still believed in him, despite their previous transgressions. Maybe even current.

Luke sighed. "I know you don't want to talk about anything else, but I want you to know, I care deeply for your sister. I wouldn't be here if I didn't."

"I just don't get why you didn't tell me about your … relationship. I wouldn't have liked it, but eventually I would've gotten used to it."

"We were going to, then I kind of messed things up." He didn't dare go into too much detail. Though he suspected Nate already knew, it wasn't necessary to provide information on his private life with Ezzie.

"Well … if she gets knocked in the head or something and decides to give you a second chance, please be straight with me about it. I won't like it, but at least I'll be aware."

Did he tell him she had done that? Hmm, he couldn't say if he was getting a second chance. They'd made love, but that didn't constitute a second chance. He really had to talk to Ezzie before he jumped on that train.

"I hope she gives me another chance. Not just so I can be there for our son, but because I really love her. I want to be with her."

Nate groaned. "Sorry, it's just going to take some getting used to. Accepting that my nephew is your son is still a little weird. Have you guys told him yet?"

"No. Though deep down I get the feeling some part of him knows. Hell, almost everyone else does."

Luke gripped the back of his neck. That was only partially true. His mother was aware Joey was his blood, but she made it clear his father had no idea. His father would be as shocked as he was finding out he had a son.

"I wouldn't go that far. I mean, yeah, my mom knows. My father on the other hand, he was as in the dark as I was, and he was pretty upset about it."

"Wait a minute? Your mom knew?"

Was it a female thing? Ezzie, her mom and his mom knew about his son before he did. There was so much wrong with that picture. He had to have a serious conversation with Ezzie about all of this.

"Yeah. Not that I'm surprised by it. She's always had some wicked sixth sense going on. I bet she even knew you and Ezzie were..." Nate trailed off and cleared his throat a couple of times. "...dating. Sorry."

Covering his mouth, Luke stifled a chuckle. Obviously, this wasn't an easy topic for his business partner. He shouldn't be amused by the guy's struggles, but he couldn't help himself. At least, not too much.

"I get it. This is your sister. We can stop talking about it."

"Oh, thank god. I mean, I appreciate you being honest with me, but I ... yeah ... I just ... I don't even want to go there."

"As long as we're good, man. That's important to me."

If they weren't, they'd manage. They had to work together. The firm kind of belonged to them in an equal partnership.

"We're good. Make sure you keep me up with my sister's case, that's all I ask."

"I'll do that."

He would've updated him the next time he reached out. As Ezzie's brother, Nate deserved his respect. As his business partner and best friend, he deserved more. Luke wouldn't take advantage of that again.

eight

"MOMMY, LOOK AT IT!" HER son pointed to the cheetah pacing back and forth in its habitat.

"I think she's stalking you. Like you'd make a great snack." Ezzie tickled the sides of her son's belly.

Squealing, he backed away and ran a little further along toward the end of the enclosure.

"Is he going to do that with every single animal here?" Luke asked.

He'd shown up on her doorstep just as she and Joey were leaving for the zoo. She'd forgotten all about teacher planning day, which cancelled school for the kids. Though she wondered what teachers had to plan about pre-school. Did they have to decide on a time for naps? Or recess?

If nothing else, it gave her and Luke time to spend together with their son that didn't revolve around food or bedtime.

Ezzie grinned. "Just the cats. He loves watching them."

"Does he think they're big play toys?"

She snickered. She'd never asked. Then again, she figured her son was four and a lot of things amused the hell out of him. "Hey, he could. Not that I'd let him bring one home."

"Ha, ha."

"Mommy, it's going away." Joey pointed at the tiger heading back into its cave.

"Well, you probably scared it off with all your gawking," Ezzie teased. She'd grown accustomed to this little tête-à-tête. Her son was too young to understand tigers, or animals period, didn't hang around for entertainment. They did what they wanted, when they wanted.

Joey crossed his arms and harrumphed. In a screechy, whiny voice he complained loudly. "Make it come baacckk."

She studied his little face. They hadn't been at the zoo more than an hour, but he hadn't eaten much for breakfast that morning. Her son had been way too excited over going to his favorite place. He was probably hungry. Hunger had a way of turning her son into an annoying tiny monster.

"Tell you what. Why don't we head over to the World of Birds Theater and you can snack on some animal crackers while we wait for the show?"

He canted his head and nodded. "Okay. I'll race ya."

Before she had a chance to respond, her son took off for the theater. She didn't care if he got too far ahead as long as he remained in sight. This had been something they had dealt with at least once. For the most part, he was pretty good about it, including then.

Luke looked on at Ezzie in amazement. She had that mom third eye. The one that knew when their child was in trouble, lying, doing something they shouldn't, or hungry. The interaction between her and their son reminded him of his own exchanges with his mother.

Smiling, he grasped Ezzie's hand and laced their fingers together. "That was pretty awesome."

"Thank you, but he and I have done this dance before."

"You mean to tell me it hasn't always been this easy?" He raised an eyebrow. No way. His son had been difficult at one point?

"At least not the first time around. I can't tell you the number of times I called my mom or your mom crying because I had no idea what I was doing. Sometimes, they had answers and sometimes, they just told me I'd figure it out."

Would it have made a difference if he'd been around in those moments? He wasn't sure. He didn't have any experience with children. He was an only child and hadn't hung around a lot of guys who had kids. Luke watched as their son hopped down the stairs to the second level bleacher.

He and Ezzie would've tried to find their way together if he'd been around, but in the end, their mothers would've still been involved. They wouldn't have had it any other way. Now it could change. He had an opportunity and he refused to miss it. He tugged on Ezzie's hand. "I know we only talked about me being there for him. What if I want more?"

"More? I mean, obviously we'd make arrangements for him to be in Utah with you. What else is there?"

"I want us, Ez. I want us to be together. A real family."

She stared at him with wide eyes and an open mouth as if he'd told her he wanted the Eiffel Tower. "Luke…"

"You can't tell me you don't feel the same way. Not after last night."

Their time together last night may have sealed the deal for him, but he'd been feeling it way before then. Despite his anger the first few days of her not telling him, he'd come to understand why. Now, he wanted it all.

"Last night was amazing, but I'm not ready to make any decisions. I'm still processing all of this. Can we get through my case and figure out how to tell Joey you're his father first?"

Luke gripped the back of his neck and sighed. She had a point. There'd be a lot of change involved if they decided to make another go of it. His practice was in Utah, her bakery was here. One thing at a time. He could begin by helping her find a way to tell their son the truth. It would have to be approached sensitively, but they could do it.

"Okay. I can wait. In the meantime, I'll help you with telling Joey."

If their son hadn't been sitting five feet away, she would've kissed Luke. He'd been so sweet about everything. Not just in the way he handled her case, but with their history, his discovery of Joey, and whatever was happening between them. He was being patient with all of it. He really had grown over the years. Ezzie caressed Luke's cheek.

How could she tell him how much this meant to her? Her eyes drifted to their connected hands. It wasn't all she would've liked to have done, but it would suffice … for now. She squeezed his hand. "Come on. Let's go join our son."

Luke grinned.

She bit the inside of her bottom lip as they walked down together. He was right about one thing. She wanted them to be a real family. She just wasn't ready to admit it.

Ezzie dropped in the seat next to Joey and Luke sat beside her. Ducking down, she set her son's backpack on the floor.

A bullet whizzed by her head. Without a second thought, she shifted in the bleacher and yanked Joey and Luke to the ground.

"Get down!" Luke hollered.

She hadn't heard the second shot. Several screams in the crowd covered the sound, but she knew the minute it struck. Her arm burned and began bleeding.

If she didn't know any better, she'd swear someone was trying to kill her.

"Can you just sit down for one second?"

"No. We need to think about what's best for our son." Ezzie grabbed a few more t-shirts out of the dresser drawer in Joey's bedroom. The police had shown up quickly after the shooting at the zoo, but by the time they'd arrived the shooter had been long gone.

She wasn't positive on the why, but she was fairly certain she'd been the target.

"I understand that, but do you really thinking sending him off to spend the night with Matt is in his best interest?"

"Yes. Matt and Colin are well equipped and can keep him safe." Why were they arguing over this? Why wasn't he helping her pack a bag for Joey instead of sitting on that damn race-car bed?

"We can keep him safe!"

"Christ. Keep your voice down." Ezzie paraded over to her son's bedroom door and peeked out the hallway. She could see the back of the couch from this angle. It didn't appear as if her son had moved. She'd left him there with a headset and one of his video games.

Crikey. They were not having this conversation. Shutting the door, she leaned her forehead against the doorjamb. She needed a second to collect her thoughts. This was difficult enough as it was; why was it impossible for Luke to understand this was the best option they had.

"You once told me that Matt taught you how to shoot. I'm assuming that isn't a skill you've let deteriorate, correct?"

She sighed and turned around. Every possible scenario played out in her head when she'd been in the hospital getting her wound dressed. Thankfully, the second bullet had only grazed her arm. It didn't mean there wouldn't be another attempt. And she'd be damned if she endangered their son's life.

"Yes, that's right. I have a 9MM that I keep in the top drawer of my nightstand, but I need you to think about all the possibilities. Not just what you would hope to happen."

"Are you trying to tell me you aren't confident in your abilities?"

"Not at all, but I'm not cocky either. I know that even a well-trained weapons expert can miscalculate and end up killed. What if that happened to me? What if, by chance, whoever this shooter was manages to sneak in here undetected and kill me? What do you think would happen to Joey?"

She desperately wanted to be positive, but she had to be realistic. Their son was four-years-old. If the shooter managed to kill her, their son's survival wouldn't be left to chance.

Luke hopped to his feet. "Then we can all go back to my hotel suite. Or get you a room at the hotel."

"And exactly how long do you think we'd be able to hide out there? Because that's what we'd have to do. I wouldn't be able to risk taking him out with us and we still have my case, possibly trial, to resolve."

She had considered that as a viable option until she weighed the issues, like how they'd have to explain to their son why they were staying in the hotel, or why he couldn't go outside and play.

"I could ask for a continuance."

"Do you think you'd get that?" She didn't know much about the law, but she suspected unless they could prove the shooting was associated to her case, the trial would proceed as scheduled. There wouldn't be any other reason to postpone her trial date.

Dropping a hand to his hip, he rubbed his eyes and groaned. "Probably not."

Ezzie bit the inside of her cheek. She could see the strain and worry in his chocolate-brown eyes. Closing the distance between them, she cupped his cheeks in both her hands. "Listen to me. I know you're apprehensive about this, but I swear to you this is our best choice."

Kissing her forehead, Luke hugged her. "You're right. I just hate the idea of him not being with us."

"I know. Me too."

"Are you sure you want to work?" Luke asked.

They'd taken up a spot on the floor in the living room of his hotel suite with her financial records in front of them. Ezzie had been antsy since they'd gotten there a half hour ago. No, wait; that wasn't right. She'd been like this since they dropped their son of with Matt and Colin.

Talk about awkward. She'd spent most of the time talking to Colin. Matt hadn't said much of anything, which shocked the hell out of him. He'd asked about it on their way to his hotel, but all Ezzie would say was that she and Matt had gotten into a fight. Great way to make him feel comfortable leaving their son there.

"Yes. It'll help distract me."

"You said that yesterday." And it hadn't done any good. The explosion had rattled her and this was a more direct threat.

Her fiery blue gaze shifted to him and intensified. "This is different. Our son could've been hurt, so believe me; I'm committed to finding some long overdue answers."

He had no argument. It was clear she was going to do what was necessary to solve this puzzle. If they were going to spend the next couple of hours digging through bank statements, then she had to tend to her bullet wound in the process.

Luke stood. "Fine, but switch places with me. I'm going to get you some pillows to elevate your arm."

"I'm fine where I'm at."

Disregarding her protest, he disappeared into the bedroom and grabbed two pillows. She could object all she wanted, but it wouldn't prevent him from taking care of her. "Just remember I'm as stubborn as you are."

How could she forget? He'd proven it over and over again this last week. But the last thing she needed was for him to play doctor. His job was lawyer, nothing else. Ezzie got to her feet and followed after him into the bedroom.

She opened her mouth and snapped it shut. Her eyes settled on Luke's ass as he bent over the bed picking up a pillow. Heat coursed through her veins. Chewing on her bottom lip, she tilted her head. Maybe he was right. Maybe she wasn't relaxed enough to sift through bank records.

God, she was horrible. Instead of focusing on evidence, sex ran rampant across her brain. Ezzie sauntered toward him. "There is another way I can be distracted."

"Oh?" He looked up from his position over the bed and mouthed a silent *oh*. Luke met her halfway and ran a hand through her tresses.

Closing her eyes, she let the sensation of his touch relax her overworked nerves. It was minor, but she loved the feel of his hand in her hair.

He brushed a soft kiss across her lips and rested his forehead against hers. "Are you sure?"

"Very."

"What about your arm?" Luke caressed the nape of her neck.

She bit her bottom lip and smiled. The doctor had only said to keep it clean and elevated. That was *exactly* what she intended to do.

Ezzie lifted her arms in the air. "I guess you better keep it above my head."

He loved the woman who stood in front of him and hated how she knew exactly which buttons to push. Luke pulled her t-shirt over her head and tossed it aside. Covering her mouth with his, he stroked her bottom lip and nipped her tongue.

Moaning into the kiss, Ezzie brought her arms around his neck and ran her fingers through his short brown hair.

Fuck, that sound. A jolt of electricity shot down to his dick. She might as well have purred in his ear. Skating his fingers up and down her spine, he unbuttoned and unzipped her jeans. He trailed kisses along her jaw and neck, then continued to her collarbone.

Unhooking her bra, he let it fall to the floor and followed the path created by her body. Kneading one of her breasts, he sucked on the nipple of the other.

She fisted a handful of his hair and dug her nails into his shoulder.

He groaned and swirled his tongue around the other nipple. They both deserved attention. Tracing more kisses down her abdomen, he squeezed her ass and slowly pulled her jeans off one leg at a time.

Rising back to his full height, Luke grabbed Ezzie by the ass and hoisted her off the ground. Her lips crashed against his. Their tongues entangled and his cock hardened. God, what she did to him. He couldn't wait long to be buried deep inside of her. Although they'd made love three times the night before, he could never get enough.

The friction created between his t-shirt and her bare breasts made her nipples pucker. Fuck, she needed him. Hooking her legs around his waist, she gyrated against his hips. Even with his pants still on, his rigid shaft rubbed the right spot through her panties.

Luke lowered her onto the bed and yanked his own t-shirt off.

"God, yes!" Ezzie moaned. Her yearning for him had increased tenfold in the last twenty-four hours. She asked for a distraction, but it was more than that. The shooting had reminded her how fragile life was and that it should be cherished.

Having Luke there, back in her life, she'd been presented with another chance. A chance to love him the way he deserved. A chance to bring their family together. A chance she'd been dreaming of for a long time.

A chance she'd been afraid would never happen.

Sliding a finger insider her wet folds, Luke latched onto a breast and loosened his jeans.

Balling the comforter in her hand, ragged breaths escaped her mouth. Her lower belly tightened and she rocked against his finger. She was so close.

Luke climbed off of her, removed his jeans and boxers and peeled her panties down her legs. Spreading her legs, he got back on top of her and pressed the head of his dick to her entrance.

Ezzie lazily skimmed her fingers over the back of his neck and stared up at him. His dark brown eyes glowed. This wasn't like anything she'd seen before. She thought back to a couple of nights earlier. The words he'd said to her. *I'm still in love with you.*

At that moment, she knew he meant it.

His naked chest against hers, Luke tucked a few loose strands of Ezzie's hair behind her ear. He looked into her sparkling blue eyes. They had the most beautiful coloring; something he'd never noticed before. They were almost iridescent.

He didn't know what was going through her mind, but if he had to guess based on the way her eyes shined, he'd say she loved him. Amongst other parts of his body, his heart swelled.

Locking her lips with his, he slowly deepened the kiss and eased his cock inside her slick folds until he was buried deep in her core. Until then, he hadn't taken his time, but now he was exactly where he longed to be.

Ezzie stroked his hip with her leg and gradually rocked her hips against his.

He pistoned in and out of her. Eventually they met each other's momentum. His balls tensed, but he wasn't ready to come. Luke pulled out and drove back inside her.

"Oh god!" she cried out.

Her walls tightened around him.

It was too soon. He took his dick out of her hot cocoon and thrusted back into her. The reprieve was brief, but it was enough to intensify the burn. Not that he was sure he could take much more.

Hooking his arms beneath her shoulders, Luke drilled into her again.

His cell phone rang.

She wrapped her legs around his ass and rolled her hips. Ezzie raked her nails across his shoulder blades. Arching her back, she pushed her breasts into his chest and moaned. Her core clenched around him.

"Oh god, Luke! I'm coming!"

"Fuck, Ezzie!" That was it, he was done for. He pounded into her over and over and over. His balls contracted and he came in an explosion.

Breathing heavily, he laid his forehead in the crook of Ezzie's neck. He could fill the sheen of her sweat mixed with his own.

Inhaling and exhaling a few ragged breaths, Ezzie ran her hand up and down the back of his head. "Is it just me or did your phone ring?"

Ding!

"Yep. Sounds like whoever called left a message." But he was in no hurry to listen to it. He didn't want to move.

"Should we see who it was?" She draped her arm across his back. Her fingers lightly skimmed over his shoulder.

Yes, but I'm perfectly content just lying here. Checking the missed call log and listening to the voicemail wasn't high on his priority list. Too bad it couldn't wait forever. Or even until tomorrow. It had to be important if they had left a message.

Luke reached over to the nightstand and grabbed his phone. "It's my P.I."

"Maybe he found something."

He nodded. Dialing his P.I., he put it on speaker phone.

It rang once before being answered. "Hey, Luke."

"Hey, Howard. What's going on?" Yeah, he hadn't heard the voicemail, but he didn't need to. His P.I. wouldn't have left anything detailed that way. It would've been a simple *call me back.*

"I did a deep dive like you asked me to and you're not going to believe what I turned up. Your suspicions were dead on."

Ezzie frowned. His suspicions? What had Luke suspected? And why hadn't he shared them with her?

Luke glanced at her, and then returned his attention to the phone. "What'd you find?"

"Jonathan Burke isn't Jonathan Burke. He's Wallace Anderson and a big-time conman. The guy has warrants in three other states. Jonathan Burke is really an accountant, but he's eighty-years-old and retired."

Her eyes widened. How was that possible? Eighty-years-old? Retired? No. It had to be wrong. All wrong. His picture ... she blinked. It had been blank. The website hadn't housed a photograph, just the name and CPA number. Shit. She *had* been played for a fool.

"What about Veronica O'Reilly?" Luke asked.

"Her identity is valid, but she's connected to Mr. Anderson. They were dating. I've located her, but not him. I'm staking her place out as we speak."

"Thanks, Howard. Keep me updated."

"Will do." The call ended.

Not only had Jonathan ... Wallace ... whatever his name was ... fooled her, but he'd been hooking up with his secretary right under her nose. Explained why Veronica portrayed her and forged all of her signatures. Tears prickled the corner of her eyes.

"Hey, now. None of that." Luke wiped the tears away.

"I feel so stupid."

He caressed her cheek. "Ez, you're the smartest woman I know. This guy took advantage of your trust. That's what conmen do. What do you say we do everything we can to ensure he doesn't do it to someone else?"

She kissed the inside of his hand and shifted her gaze to him. *I really do love him.* He had known exactly what to say and how to get her motivated.

Ezzie brushed a tender kiss across his lips. "Let's kick some ass."

"That's my girl."

nine

LUKE WRENCHED HIS DARK BLUE denim jeans up over his legs. Buttoning them up, he peered at the beautiful woman lying in his bed and smiled. She was still passed out cold. After Howard's call the night before, he and Ezzie had scoured through all of the bank statements.

They'd found the transfers she had previously mentioned. Small amounts had been relocated beginning about six months after she'd taken Jonathan on as an accountant. It equaled close to two hundred thousand dollars over the last two and half years. Although the money had been transferred in lump sums, they occurred in larger amounts after significant deposits had been made into the bakery's account. He confirmed it all lined up to monies received from the investment companies where Ezzie's signature had been forged.

The account the funds had been moved to had only been identified as Love LLC. There'd been no other information on the account or what the money had been used for. Part of the discovery in evidence indicated Ezzie had been the account holder for Love LLC. The application for the account or the Tax ID number associated with it hadn't been included in evidence. He'd have to issue a subpoena to get those records. He suspected those documents had been forged as well.

He hadn't heard anything more from his private investigator on any movement of Veronica O'Reilly. But Ezzie had said she was certain she lived close to her bakery. The woman shouldn't be too hard to find. Shoving his socked feet into his sneakers, Luke placed a soft kiss on Ezzie's forehead.

It had been a long night, so he had no plans on waking her up. She earned the right to sleep in. He walked back into the living room and spotted her car keys on the coffee table. Hmm, should he just take her Jeep? He didn't intend to be gone long.

Snagging the keys, he scribbled a quick note, then left the hotel suite and headed downstairs to the attached parking garage. If his memory served him correctly, the bakery was only about twenty minutes from the hotel. The drive from Ezzie's apartment building to that coffee house that was across the street from her bakery had taken fifteen minutes and his taxi ride to her place from the hotel had taken less than five.

Luke climbed into the Jeep, readjusted the seat and accessed directions up on GPS. He'd learned a few of the streets in Los Angeles, but he was still definitely finding his way around.

Tapping his fingers against the steering wheel, he backed the Jeep up and exited the parking garage. Despite everything finally coming together in Ezzie's case, he had yet to figure out how they could tell Joey he was his father without breaking his son's heart. How could they explain why he'd been absent all this time?

Will you tell me a story about one of my daddy's rescues? That's right. Their son had called his cases rescues. That was it. That was how they could explain it. All of his clients had required his help. He and Ezzie could tell their son that those people needed him and that he knew his son would be in good hands with his mother. Luke grinned.

If his son was older that probably wouldn't work, but with him being so young ... it would be the perfect explanation. There was no reason to state he'd only learned of his existence a week ago.

His cell phone rang. He glanced at the caller ID. Finally! IT had had Ezzie's computer for almost a week. "Hey Jake, tell me what you got."

"A frigging doozy. I just want you to know that after this mess, you owe me. That USB was a virus. Its intention was to wipe everything completely out. It did a damn good job too."

"Are you saying you couldn't recover anything?" This guy was supposed to be the best. They'd used him a couple of times and so far, they'd had good luck. He really hoped it hadn't run out.

"I didn't say that. It just took me longer than expected. Most of everything was fried, but I managed to extract a few files. It wasn't much, but it had to do with an account for Love LLC. I sent them to your tablet."

That's what he was talking about. God, let this be the last bit of proof they needed to clear Ezzie's name. Luke slowed the Jeep and parked alongside the curb in front of the bakery. "You're awesome, man."

"It's what I do. Let me know if you need anything else."

"Thanks, Jake."

Luke hung up the phone and shut off the ignition. He climbed out of the car, closed the door and eyeballed the building in front of him. It had a hand-painted cupcake with And Dessert Too written in curlicue letters on the glass door. From there he could see the empty display case.

He hated seeing Ezzie's bakery so dismal. It looked ... lonely. Shaking his head, he eyed the surrounding buildings and the cars parked on the street. There were a few possibilities for apartments, but what he was really searching for was Howard's truck. It would pinpoint exactly where he had to go.

Walking around the front of the Jeep, Luke stepped off the sidewalk and started across the street.

Kaboom!

The bakery exploded and sent him flying. He landed hard on the ground. Car alarms blared. Glass from nearby vehicles and the bakery shattered and rained down all around him.

With a groan, Luke attempted to lift his head so he could gather his bearings, but he couldn't move. He blinked. The sky blurred and darkness claimed him.

Finished with her hair, Ezzie turned the blow-dryer off. Her cell phone rang again. She'd heard it when she first began drying her hair, but figured it could wait. This had to be at least the second time someone had tried to get a hold of her. Maybe a third. What was so important?

She picked up her phone, but didn't catch the call in time. Pulling up her call log, she scanned the missed calls. One call was from an unknown number. Her brother had called four times. They hadn't spoken in days. Ezzie went to return his call when her phone rang again.

"Hi—"

"Where the hell have you been? I've been trying to get a hold of you for ten minutes now!"

"I'm sorry, I was—"

"Never mind, it's not important. Luke's in the hospital. You need to go, now."

"What!? What happened?" She raced across the room, slipped on a pair of sneakers and scanned the coffee table for her car keys. That's where she remembered leaving them. Where were they?

"I don't know much, just that there was an explosion and he got caught in it."

"Explosion? Oh god! Is he alive? Tell me he's alive." Ezzie froze. No, no, no. This had to be a bad dream. She couldn't get him back only to lose him all over again. She swallowed and inhaled a deep breath. She had to focus on finding her keys. It was the only way she would get answers.

"He's alive, but it's…" her brother paused. "I just don't know how bad it is."

"You said he was at a hospital. What hospital?" Shit. Where were her damn keys? Ezzie moved the pillows around on the couch, knelt down and looked underneath it.

"Dignity Health. What are you doing? Are you leaving?"

"I can't find my—" Her eyes landed on the note on the coffee table. Damn it. Left her with two options and one was likely faster than other. "Shit! He took my keys. I'll get to the hospital. I'll call you when I find out something."

"You do that. I'm on the next flight to California."

She swallowed. If her brother was hopping on a plane to get there, it was bad. It was really bad. Tears rolled down her cheeks. *This is no time for crying.* Wiping her face, she sniffled. No matter how bad it was, her brother would be there. Whether for her, Luke or both of them she didn't know. Either way, she was grateful.

"Nate, thank you."

"You're welcome. Now, go on and get to the hospital. I'll see you soon."

Briefly nodding, Ezzie disconnected the line and called Matt. They weren't really talking, but they'd both have to get past that for now. She truly needed him.

Matt, Colin, Ezzie, and Joey all rushed into the emergency room entrance and stopped. Matt had never been to this particular hospital before. Not that he had visited many in his life. Still, how did they begin to find out where in the hospital Luke was located? It was a decent sized campus.

Holding up a finger, Ezzie approached the front desk and spoke with a nurse there for a moment. She returned to their little group. "He's in the trauma center in Leavey Hall, the next building over. Come on, let's go."

Of all the things he had ever wanted for his best friend, this was not one of them. Yeah, he'd done a couple of things he wasn't proud of to keep her and Luke apart. But he sure as hell didn't want the guy dead.

They all followed after Ezzie to the building on the other side of the parking garage. This time they all walked up to the nurse's station.

"I'm looking for Luke Jonnihan. I got a call he was here," Ezzie said.

The nurse tapped a few things on her computer. "Are you family?"

"Yes, I'm his wife."

"Do you have proof? Driver's license? Marriage certificate?" The nurse asked.

Married? When the fuck had that happened? First, she sleeps with him while he's babysitting, then they hit an altar while Joey was, again, in his care. Had Ezzie lost her marbles? Matt opened his mouth.

Colin squeezed his forearm and gently shook his head.

Fine. He'd keep his trap shut, for the time being. Matt frowned.

"We just recently got married. I haven't changed my information yet. My brother, Nathan Donovan, is his one of his emergency contacts. He called me and told me he was here. I also got a voicemail from someone here at the hospital. I can give you whatever information you need, but I want to see him," Ezzie calmly stated.

"Mrs. Jonnihan, I apologize, but he's not able to be seen at the moment. If you can take these forms with you to the waiting room and give us any information about his past medical history, I'll let his doctors know you're here."

Forms? They wanted her to fill out fucking forms? Screw the goddamn forms. She needed to know he was okay. Ezzie inhaled and exhaled a deep breath. It took everything she had in her not to strangle this nurse. "Fine, but you get that doctor or any doctor that can tell me what's going on pronto."

"Yes, ma'am." The nurse handed her a clipboard full of forms and a pen.

Great. Ezzie turned to her friends and son.

Matt's eyes narrowed at her. He glanced from her to his boyfriend. "Why don't you take Joey down to the vending machine and get some drinks for everyone?"

Colin looked to Ezzie and she nodded.

Obviously, Matt was pissed at her again but she wasn't in the mood to deal with his personal issues.

Taking her son's hand, Colin disappeared down the hallway.

Ezzie headed over to the waiting room and proceeded to fill out everything she could accurately answer about Luke. Good thing they'd talked about what had been missed in the last five years. Not to mention she'd been keeping track of him all this time. That combined with their history, she should be able to answer just about everything.

"Care to tell me when you got married?"

She glimpsed over her shoulder to Matt and lowered her voice. "We haven't, but I knew it was the only way they were going to tell me anything."

"Is this kind of like when you didn't mean to have sex? It's not like there aren't twenty-four-hour wedding chapels around here."

"Whether we did or not, what the hell is your problem? He's my son's father and I happen to be in love with him." She knew he'd done something to keep her and Luke apart before, but she didn't believe Matt would be so angry over them trying to work things out.

"My problem is that everything he has done in the past to prove he isn't good enough for you and you still act like a love-sick puppy. He did you worse than Justin and yet you've still forgiven him."

Oh hell no. Ezzie couldn't believe Matt had had the nerve to bring in her ex-boyfriend prior to Luke. Justin had done her wrong by actually cheating. She'd caught him having sex with someone else. Luke ... he hadn't done anything of the sort. The kiss had been explained and she'd accepted it as the truth.

"You know as well as I do that's a load of crap. Luke didn't abandon me. You convinced him I had moved on. And he still kept calling me, but he had my old number. It was convenient how I lost my phone and you offered to get me a new one with a brand-new number. You have anything to do with my missing phone?"

"That's not the point."

"Then what is? Because all I keep hearing is how you continuously got between us."

She had scoffed at the one time Luke asked if Matt could've been secretly in love with her. Her best friend had been as gay back then as he was now. This overactive desire to keep her and Luke apart made no sense.

"Everything I have ever done has been to keep you and my godson safe. Hiding your phone, sending Luke back to Massachusetts, stealing that USB from Jonathan. All of it. And this is the thanks I get." Matt violently slashed his hand at her.

Ezzie's eyes widened. She hadn't imagined he'd really do something so dumb or childish. Her phone, Luke ... and what USB was he talking about? Okay. She had to address these one at a time. "Luke is Joey's father. Last I checked, godfather didn't trump father. And what—"

"Mommy?"

Rubbing her eyes, she hung her head. Shit. How much of that had her son heard? Ezzie spun on the ball of her foot.

Joey's bottom lip trembled. Tears rolled down his cheeks. "Is Luke ... is he my daddy?"

Fuck, this was not how she planned to tell him the truth. But she couldn't lie to him directly now that he'd heard it. Ezzie clutched the clipboard tightly against her hip. "Yes."

Her son didn't wait for her to say anything else. He turned around and ran out of the waiting room crying.

Shit, shit, shit. She started after her son—

"Mrs. Jonnihan?"

Damn it. Not now. Ezzie looked between the waiting room exit and the doctor.

Colin, who had been lingering nearby, hooked a thumb over his shoulder and took off in the direction her son had gone.

One problem temporarily solved. God knew how many more to go. Ezzie sighed and focused her attention on the doctor. "Yes, I'm Mrs. Jonnihan."

"I'm one of your husband's doctors, Dr. Jeffries."

"How is he? Can I see him?"

Those were the most important questions she had. Once she had those answered, she could try getting a hold of her brother. Wait, she also had to figure out what the hell Matt had been referring to.

"He's in surgery. We don't know much yet, just that the explosion lacerated his liver and there's some other internal injuries we're still ascertaining. Does he have any allergies we need to be aware of? Or any past surgeries?"

Lacerated liver? Internal bleeding? None of that was good. He probably had a lot more scrapes and bruises than what her brother had left him with. Ezzie swallowed. This was bad. Really bad. God, she couldn't lose him.

"Mrs. Jonnihan?"

She blinked. Right. He had asked about allergies and surgeries. "He, uh, penicillin. He's allergic to penicillin. And he's only had one surgery. He broke his ankle skiing when he was sixteen."

The doctor jotted some notes. "Thank you. I'll let you know as soon as we know more."

"Thank you. I appreciate it."

"Of course." Dr. Jeffries left.

Shit. She had to do something. Otherwise, she'd wind up pacing the tiny waiting room for however long Luke was back there.

Surgery could take time, but how much time? Ezzie bit the inside of her cheek. One thing at a time, right? If she stayed here, she'd be playing the waiting game. If she figured out what Matt had been talking about, then maybe she could find a way to be useful. And figure out what happened to Luke in the process. With a game plan, she glared at Matt.

"What USB?"

Ten

OF ALL THE IDIOTIC THINGS her best friend could do. And she thought her borrowing the key for her accountant's office was bad. But to outright break into someone's home and steal shit? He was fucking crazy. Ezzie groaned to herself as she let herself into Matt's apartment.

She'd left him at the hospital with Colin and her son. She had to insist he tell her exactly where he'd hidden the USB. According to him, it should be on his desk, which meant it could be buried under his latest fashion design. Crikey. Why couldn't he have stayed out of everything?

Closing the door, Ezzie strolled down the hallway to the spare bedroom, the one Matt had turned into his office once she'd moved out. She surveyed the high-top desk he had, which was covered in several designs in various stages. She lifted the papers, opened drawers, but didn't see anything.

Maybe it wasn't in there at all. She headed to Matt's bedroom and checked the middle drawer first. It had always been his junk drawer. A mass had accumulated over the years in it. She dug through miscellaneous items like unmarked keys, manuals for electronic devices, and a multitude of other things. Nothing.

She pulled out the top drawer, which was where Matt kept his gun.

Only his 9MM and bullets were in there.

That's when she heard it. The distinct clicking sound the cocking of a gun makes. "Looking for this?"

Ezzie turned around.

Her accountant stood in the bedroom doorway holding up a black USB and pointing a gun in her direction. "You couldn't make this easy, could you? All you had to do was take the fall, but you had to play detective."

She had never seen him shoot and he'd never mentioned it. But she couldn't act as if he had no clue what he was doing. Even if he didn't, he could get lucky. Ezzie scrutinized the gun in his hand. Did she have a chance at grabbing Matt's 9MM? The drawer was still open.

"I'm sorry, Jonathan. It's not in my nature to roll over and play dead. Or should I say Wallace?"

"You know about that, huh? That's too bad. I kind of liked you. I mean, I wish that thug had better aim. Or that your boyfriend hadn't gone looking for Veronica. Tsk, tsk, tsk."

"The explosion at my bakery? That was you? Why?"

He'd been a real monster this whole time. Using her as a fall guy. Blowing up his own house. Trying to have her killed. Then destroying her bakery. For what? Money?

"Honestly, I figured if I took away your bakery, you'd stop fighting and just go with the flow. You know, accept your fate."

"My fate?" Based on what she could see of the gun, it was a 45. semi-automatic. The safety was off. A 45 packed a decent punch and he was a scrawny guy. Didn't mean he couldn't control the weapon. Ezzie eyed the open drawer out of her periphery. She wouldn't likely get to the gun before Jonathan got a shot off.

"Yes. And it's brought us—"

The front door opened and Matt walked in. "Ezzie, I'm really sorry about everything. I've been kind of an ass about the whole Luke thing."

Jonathan glanced over his shoulder.

Ezzie didn't hesitate. She grabbed the gun out of Matt's drawer, switched

off the safety, aimed and shot until her accountant fell to the floor.

"Jesus Christ!" Matt ran down the hall to his bedroom where all the shooting had come from. He skidded to a halt just outside his bedroom door.

Ezzie stood there with his gun in her hand just staring.

Her account was sprawled out on the floor bleeding from two different holes, but he was still breathing. A 45 lay not too far from the guy.

"Is he … is he…" Ezzie paused and swallowed. "Is he dead?"

"No."

Which was probably a good thing. He couldn't imagine how she'd feel knowing she killed a man. Kicking the 45. away from Jonathan, Matt dug his cell phone out of his pocket and dialed 9-1-1.

"9-1-1, what's your emergency?"

"An intruder's been shot in my apartment. Send an ambulance to 550 North Figueroa Street, Apartment 759." *Think, think, think.* He had to stop the bleeding, but he couldn't take a chance Jonathan would get back up. The gun was out of reach. Speaking of gun, Matt eyeballed his best friend.

Ezzie still stood there pointing the gun toward him and the door. "I shot him."

"An ambulance is on its way, sir."

"Please hurry." Matt hung up phone and tucked it back in his pocket. He snagged his pink, fuzzy handcuffs off the hook attached to his dresser. Crouching down, he placed them on Jonathan's wrists, and then slowly made his way to his best friend.

He kept his hands where she could see them, but purposely put himself between her and her accountant. If he was going to retrieve his weapon, he needed her to realize who it was approaching. "I need you to give me the gun, Ezzie."

She blinked and tears trickled down her cheeks. "Matt?"

"Yeah, sweetie. It's me. I need you to give me the gun." He held his hand out to her.

Laying the pistol in his hand, she collapsed into his arms and sobbed.

Matt set the weapon on his nightstand and embraced Ezzie tightly. She had to be horrified at what she'd had to do. "Shh, it's okay. I got you."

He glanced over at the guy on the floor. Jonathan looked like he'd passed out. God, he still hoped he was alive.

The blare of sirens could be heard through the window. Good. The ambulance had to be close.

"Oh god! The USB!" Ezzie unfolded herself from Matt's arms and scanned the floor.

"What?"

Kneeling down, she picked up a small black stick off the floor and held it out for him to see.

The USB he'd stolen. Shit. Her accountant had been a real bad guy. *Guess there was a reason I never trusted him.*

"Hello? Paramedics!"

"Back here!" Matt called out. He wrapped an arm around Ezzie's shoulder and they both stood off to the side. He expected police would be there shortly too.

This was going to be a very long night.

"What the hell happened?"

"Is that blood on your shirt? Where's Luke?"

"You got arrested? Why would you hide that from us?"

Ezzie's gaze shifted from her brother to Luke's parents to her parents. All five of them surrounded her and each of them spouted a different question at her simultaneously. "Stop it! I can't answer you all at once. One at a time, please."

They all started up again.

She pinched the bridge of her nose. This wasn't working. Ezzie threw her hands up. "Enough!"

Children. She'd have to treat them like children to answer their questions. It had been a long day already. This was the last thing she wanted to be doing, but she understood their positions. At least they were the only ones in the waiting room. Thank God for small favors.

Ezzie pointed to Luke's parents. "You first."

"What is going on with my son? Where is he?" Luke's mother asked.

"He's in the ICU. There was an explosion at my bakery that he got caught in. His organs suffered a lot of damage that caused some internal bleeding. The doctors were able to stop that and repair his organs, but he's still critical."

A lacerated liver, torn colon, and perforated lung hadn't been the worst Luke had suffered. About an hour ago, the doctors had induced a coma due to some swelling on his brain. But he was a fighter. She just had to keep reminding herself of that.

Luke's mother gasped. "An explosion? How is that even possible? Who would do that?"

Do I really need to go into all that? There had to be a shorter way to answer that, unless the question was entirely rhetorical. Ezzie chewed the inside of her cheek. Who was she kidding? The woman never asked anything she didn't want answered.

"I don't want to go into all the details, but he was trying to protect me."

"Does it have something to do with your arrest?" Nate asked.

Why did that seem like an even longer response? Ezzie blew out a deep breath. "Yes. It has everything to do with it."

"Arrest? Is that what he was here for?" Luke's father said.

"Yes. He was here to defend me. My accountant embezzled money from me by forging my signature on contracts with investors. And he set me up to take the fall. Luke and I have been working all week trying to find evidence to prove my innocence."

At least she'd been able to summarize it all, even if she had left out a few key components. But did they really have to know about the first explosion? Or that they'd been shot at?

Her father cocked an eyebrow. "How did all of that lead to your bakery blowing up?"

If she went by what Jonathan told her, she'd ruined his plans and he was trying to take whatever he could away from her. Yeah. She didn't think any of them would accept that, even if it was mostly true.

"My accountant started doing whatever he could to hurt me. Listen, I know you guys want me to explain everything. And I will, I promise. Right now, I just want to be in the room with Luke. I don't want him to be alone if he wakes up."

"When." Luke's mother grasped Ezzie's hands and squeezed. "*When* he wakes up. I know he's going to pull through. Esmeralda, he loves you too much not to fight."

"I love him too. I can't imagine…" Ezzie paused. That wasn't right. She refused to think like that. "I don't want to lose him."

"Beverly's right. Luke is a strong young man and he's going to be fine. I just wish you had told us everything so we could've been there for you both." Her mother offered her a lopsided smile.

"I'm sorry I didn't. I thought it was the only way I could protect Joey."

She should've known none of them would've told him about her arrest. Not that he would've understood even if they had.

Ezzie hugged her parents. "I'm glad you guys are here."

"You too." She extended her arm to Luke's mother who joined in on the group hug, followed by her brother and finally Luke's father.

Ezzie felt a feathered touch on her shoulder. The sensation caused her to bolt upright in the chair she'd occupied for the last five days. Her gaze settled on Luke. His eyes were still closed. He'd stirred a bit in the last few hours, at least long enough the doctors had been able to remove the tube from his throat, but he hadn't fully awakened yet. For a second, she thought—

"Sorry to wake you, but Detective Jacobs is outside waiting to talk to us," Matt said.

Ezzie shifted her gaze to her best friend. Matt hadn't left her side since the shooting. He'd really been there for her, which had given them ample time to talk about his intervention. While she didn't like what he'd done, in the end she'd understood why.

His incessant apologizing had helped a little, though she had made it quite clear he'd have to seek Luke's forgiveness too. She suspected that was part of the reason Matt had hung around the hospital room. Not that she believed he'd bombard Luke the second he came around.

"I'll be out in a second."

"Okay." Matt stepped out of the hospital room.

Turning her attention back to her other half, Ezzie brushed some of Luke's hair from his face. It was one of the few places not covered in bruises or stitches. A lot of the damage had been internal, but that didn't mean the outside hadn't come through unscathed. His abdomen looked like he'd gone a few rounds with Mike Tyson. Both of his arms were bandaged or stitched where he'd been hit with shrapnel or cut by shards of glass.

Despite all that, no major arteries had been knicked and the internal injuries had been repairable. His body had taken a beating, but he was healing a little every day. She reminded herself of that every time she looked at him.

Ezzie stood and pressed a tender kiss to Luke's forehead. She glanced at their son. "I need to go talk to the police officer for a moment. Will you be okay by yourself?"

"Yes, Mommy." Joey had refused to leave his father's side almost as much as she had. No matter how hard she'd tried to get him to wait with her's or Luke's parents, he just kept saying he had to be there.

"Okay. Holler at me if your dad wakes up." She placed a kiss against Joey's head and slipped out of the hospital room.

"Ms. Donovan, Mr. Harris, thank you for joining me. I promise to make this quick."

Leaving the door open a crack, Ezzie nodded and glimpsed over her shoulder. She was going to hold him to that. Hopefully, it didn't mean he'd just come there to arrest her. That would definitely not be quick.

Matt angled himself so he stood somewhat between her and Detective Jacobs. His positioning hadn't gone unnoticed, at least by her, and more than likely the detective.

Ezzie bit the inside of her cheek. *God, please don't let this be a sign.* She gave Detective Jacobs her full attention. "I presume you have news."

"Yes, ma'am. We were able to gain access to that USB you discovered. That combined with the other evidence your lawyer found is proof that Wallace Anderson was the mastermind of the operation."

Ezzie blinked. This was good, right? This was exactly what she and Luke had worked so hard to accomplish. Then why didn't it feel like a weight had been lifted from her shoulders? She replayed the detective's statement in her mind. Nothing had been said about what was going to happen to her, that's why.

"Does that mean the prosecutor is dropping the charges against me?"

"Yes. We've arrested Mr. Anderson and Ms. O'Reilly. They've both made deals, but they'll be going away for a long, long time."

"Oh my god, thank you. Thank you, I—"

She had no other words. Tears prickled the corners of her eyes. She was so relieved. When Luke woke up, she could actually tell him they did it. They—

"What about the shooting?" Matt asked.

Her shoulders sagged. She bit the inside of her bottom lip. That had been the sound of the other shoe. The shooting hadn't slipped her mind, she had just buried it in the recesses of her memory. Ezzie frowned and lowered her gaze to the floor. She didn't want to think about how close she had come to killing a man, even if it had been her scum of an ex-accountant. Even if she had been protecting Matt and herself, she'd still shot someone.

"Mr. Anderson confessed to his involvement in that as well. We know it was self-defense on your end, Ms. Donovan," the detective replied.

Her eyes snapped up to the detective. Ezzie blinked. Had she heard him correctly? Had her ex-accountant really come clean? Was it really all over?

"Mommy! Daddy's awake!" Joey yelled from the doorway.

Shit. What bulldozer had run him over? His entire body ached. His abdomen throbbed. His arms felt like he'd been stung several times by a bee. There was something in his nose. What was that? Luke tried to open his eyes. Fuck. They felt so heavy.

The last thing he remembered was heading across the street to the coffee house near Ezzie's bakery. Ezzie's bakery. There was something—the explosion. Shit!

"Ez…"

He had to get to Ezzie. *Open your eyes. Come on, open your eyes, damn it.* His eyes fluttered open.

Daddy? He knew that voice. Why? Luke shifted his gaze in the voice's direction. Joey, his son. Wait, he'd called him *daddy*. But they hadn't told him yet.

He looked around. Several wires hung from his chest, his arms. All linked back to various monitors around his bed. That explained something. He was in a hospital room.

It just left a whole slew of other questions. How long had he been there? Why did his body ache all the way down to his toes? How did their son find out the truth? Where was—

Ezzie burst into the room. She rushed over to his side and brushed a kiss against his forehead. "Welcome back."

One question answered. God, she was a wonderful sight to see. No matter what had gone down at her bakery, his girl was perfectly safe.

"What…" Luke croaked out.

Was that his voice? He sounded like a dying frog. His throat was sore.

Maybe that's why he sounded so horrible.

"How about an ice chip? Might help." Ezzie held out a thin disc of ice and placed it in his mouth.

It didn't take long to melt and sure as hell felt good going down the back of his throat. Once it was gone, he tried again. He had so many questions that needed answering.

His voice squeaked, but his words came out a little easier this time around. In this case, word. Maybe it was best if he limited his vocabulary. "Explosion?"

"Yeah. You were pretty banged up." Ezzie smiled and gently stroked Luke's cheek with her thumb. There was nothing more beautiful than those chocolate-brown eyes of his. In the beginning, she hadn't been sure she'd see them again.

All the touch and go those first couple of days had been exhausting. But it was worth it for them to get there. It didn't mean there weren't obstacles ahead, but she could handle those easily. Her bakery could be rebuilt. And she'd be there for Luke's recovery. Especially now that he was awake.

"What happened?" Luke squeaked out again.

She ran her fingers across the top of his head. His question didn't surprise her, but couldn't they focus on him getting better before they—

Ezzie stared at Luke. She knew better. He wouldn't be able to think about himself until he had information. "Jonathan blew up my bakery, but he's been found and he's in jail."

"How long was I out?"

Joey giggled. "Daddy talks funny."

Luke blinked and eyed Ezzie.

He had missed a lot over the last few days. There was so much more she had to tell him, but they couldn't have this conversation with their son around. She bent down to their son. "Why don't you go to the waiting room and tell Uncle Nate the good news?"

"Okay, Mommy." Joey skipped out of the hospital room singing, "My daddy's awake."

Oh boy. She had maybe three minutes tops before their entire family demanded to see him. Ezzie sat in the chair beside the bed and took Luke's hand in her own. "You've been out five days. There was a lot of internal bleeding from a lacerated liver, a torn colon, and some lung damage. They had to stick a tube down your throat, so it's probably tender."

"And Joey?"

"He overheard me and Matt arguing about you. It came out in our fight."

Their son had been really upset with her for a day or two. Then she'd sat down and just told him a comfortable truth. His father had been rescuing other people and came home to rescue them. But they wanted to keep him safe from the bad people, so they chose to wait to tell him the truth. It had taken a little time, but Joey had finally accepted that. The police presence might've helped with that.

"Is this dream?"

"Well, if it is, I don't want to wake up." She sighed. Their last few days before the explosion had been like that. A dream where she hadn't been wrong, although she had and it was time she rectified that. "I'm so sorry about everything. I really hope you can forgive me for what I put you through."

"Forgiven, if you can forgive me."

"For what?"

What in the world would she need to forgive him for? He hadn't—that wasn't true. She had pointed out how he should've never put himself in the position to be kissed.

Luke opened his mouth.

"You're forgiven." Ezzie caressed his cheek. She brushed a soft kiss to his lips. "I love you, Luke Jonnihan. And nothing is going to keep us apart."

It felt so good to say that out loud. She hadn't been positive she'd have the chance. *God, thank you for bringing him back to me.*

"I love you, too."

"That's good, because you're kind of stuck with me."

"Wouldn't have it … any … other … way." He grinned.

"Me either." Ezzie kissed him one more time. She peered over her shoulder through the glass windows to the hallway. It was still empty, but it wouldn't stay that way for much longer. Their families had given her priority, but that didn't mean they wouldn't show their faces soon. As much as she wanted more time alone with Luke, she'd have to relinquish it for a few minutes.

Besides, they'd have plenty of that in the future.

"Listen; there are a lot of people here to see you. Before they all bombard you, I'm going to get a nurse. I know the doctor will want to come check on you." She got to her feet.

Luke tightened his grip on her hand. "Don't go."

"I promise I'll be back. I'm in for the long haul."

Six months later …

Ezzie strolled up the walk to their two-story, ranch-style home. She still couldn't believe they lived there and it had been a few months since they'd moved in. Seemed like they had just arrived yesterday.

After her bakery blew up and her accountant's arrest, the newspaper printed a new story all about what she'd faced to clear her name. Luke had been right about her reputation.

Her customers had visited the bakery often during clean-up and reconstruction. They'd even had a big party to celebrate, but it hadn't been the same. Her regulars may not have cared, but she'd felt the stain anytime she baked in that kitchen.

Luke had stayed with her in California recovering from his injuries for a couple of months while she rebuilt. During that time, they worked on their relationship and spent time together as a family.

About the time he was ready to go back to work, she'd decided a change was in order. His support made her choice easy. She left the store in the hands of her most trusted employee: Lucy. Ezzie still owned the bakery, but now she worked a bit closer to home in a second bakery. It was all part of her expansion project.

Also meant Luke didn't have to move his practice. Instead, she and Joey returned with him to Green River, Utah. It allowed them to be closer to their families.

Unlocking the door, Ezzie headed inside. "I'm home."

She peered down the hallway at a line of cupcake wrappers all along the wooden floor. What was this? Raising an eyebrow, she followed the path to her and Luke's bedroom. Quite strange. She hadn't left any cupcakes out on the kitchen counter, but someone had been into her baking supplies.

"Hello?" Ezzie called out and pushed their bedroom door open. She gasped.

Luke and their son stood in the center of the room, side by side in flamingo pink tuxedos. They looked like the icing on her favorite cake.

But that wasn't all. The entire room had been decorated. Twinkling lights hung along the walls. Pictures of her and Luke at various times in their relationship hung from the ceiling. There were photographs from their camping trip, him carrying her over his shoulder into their new home, the last restaurant he'd taken her to eat at … and so many more. Years of their time together.

It was so beautiful. Tears tickled the corners of her eyes. *Damn hormones.* Ezzie cleared her throat and pulled herself together. "What's all this?"

"Special 'casion, Mommy," Joey said.

"Oh? What's the occasion?" She shifted her gaze from their son to her boyfriend. Luke had a bright smile on his face. It was warm and a bit nerve-wracking at the same time.

Stepping forward, Luke reached for her hand and took it within his own. "I love you so much. More than I ever thought possible."

"I love you too." Oh god, he was going to make her cry again. She really didn't want to tell him her news with a tear-stained face. *Deep breath. Just take a few, slow deep breaths.*

Yep. That was exactly what she had to do.

Inhale, exhale. A couple times of that and she'd be good to go. Wait a minute, something was going on. He was staring at her and not the normal sultry way he tended to do, but the way he did when he was up to something. The way the room—her eyes landed on the big heart on their bed. It had been made out of cupcake wrappers. How had she missed that?

She swallowed. *Deep breath.*

Wow. He really didn't think he'd be this nervous. He'd been planning this day for weeks. Luke stared at the woman he loved with all of his heart.

She hadn't just given him a family, but she believed in him despite his inability to believe in himself. These last few months had shown him everything he never thought he deserved.

Ezzie had been there every day by his side through his recovery. And he couldn't imagine not having her there for the rest of his life. It was time he let that be known to the whole world.

"The last few years have been filled with a lot of bumps in the road. And we still kept going. We were broken, but never defeated."

"We're both too stubborn for that." She winked.

Their affinity to never give up had been what led them to where they stood. Her initial ultimatum. His inability to live without her in his life. The struggles from their own past that they had weathered, separately and together. The fights they'd overcome. Their refusal to never stop loving one another. It all came down to their stubbornness and he wouldn't have it any other way.

"Definitely part of what makes us work. But it was also our love and our faith in one another that got us through."

Removing a velvet box from the pocket of his slacks, Luke got down on one knee and presented a sparkling, princess-cut diamond ring. "I don't know that I'd be who I am today without you in my life. Esmeralda Marie Donovan, will you make me the happiest man in the world and be my wife?"

Her eyes widened. Tears trickled down her cheeks. She bit her bottom lip and the corners of her lips tugged into the brightest smile he'd ever seen. "Yes. Yes, I'll marry you."

"Yay!" Joey jumped up and down.

He hopped to his feet and placed the ring on her left hand. Wrapping Ezzie in his arms, Luke pressed a loving kiss to his fiancée's lips. He loved the sound of that.

Their son pumped his fist in the air and hollered. "She said yes!"

Holding onto Luke, Ezzie laughed at their son. At first, she thought he was just super excited. Then she saw her parents, her brother, and Luke's parents all come through the bedroom door.

Oh boy. Well, she hadn't planned to share the news she had to share with her—fiancée—holy shit, she was engaged! Hmm, could they plan a wedding in less than ... seven months?

"Congratulations!" Her mother hugged her. "I'm so happy for you."

"Thank you."

"Yes, congratulations, my dear." Luke's mother hugged her. "I'm so glad Lucas *finally* proposed."

"Mom!" Luke exclaimed.

"Beverly, stop teasing the boy. They're getting married now and that's what matters," Luke's father said.

Ezzie grinned. She couldn't have said it better herself.

"That you are, and I'll be proud to call you son." Her father shook Luke's hand.

She was elated to see that. It had taken her father a little time to forgive the two of them, but eventually he had.

Her brother extended a handshake to Luke. The two clasped hands. "Congrats, man. I'm happy for you, but if you hurt my sister, I will kill you."

"Nathan Marcus!" her mother yelled.

"Nate!" *For crying out loud.* The one time she would've preferred her brother act normal. Then again, this was his normal. His overbearing, overprotective normal.

"What? I'm kidding. He knows that." Nate smirked.

Luke held up a hand and silenced them all. "It's okay. I love your sister and I'm looking forward to a very long life with her."

That was the sweetest thing ever. Ezzie bit her bottom lip to keep the tears at bay. That sealed it. She was just going to tell them all at once.

She waggled her finger at their son, and then looked to her and Luke's families. "I have something to tell you all."

"News about the bakery?" Luke asked.

"Something like that." Ezzie leaned down and whispered in their son's ear, then straightened back up.

"I'm gonna be a big brother?" Joey cried out.

Luke blinked. Slowly his eyes enlarged. "Ez ... are you ... are we pregnant?"

She nodded. "Eight weeks."

"We're going to have a baby!" Throwing his arms around her again, Luke pressed another kiss to her lips.

This cued another round of *congratulations.* As she and Luke embraced everyone in both their families a second time, their son whooped and hollered.

They had a lot to celebrate. Her and Luke's impending nuptials and a new baby on the way. And she was grateful for all of it. Beaming at all the joy in the room, Ezzie hooked her arm around her fiancée's waist. "I love you, Luke."

"I love you too, Ez. I can't wait for our future." He kissed her forehead and rested a hand on her lower belly.

As their families chattered on about wedding and baby plans, Ezzie drank it all in. She regarded Luke, and then turned her attention to their son, who had wrapped his arms around Luke's waist, and she smiled. *This is what life is all about.*

They had overcome a lot of hurdles to get to that moment. Seeing her family's ecstatic faces, she wouldn't have traded it for all the stars in the sky.

Because love was worth the fight.

ABOUT THE AUTHOR

Author of the Love's Worth Series, BRIGIT ROSÉ, lives in a world of romance. She has taken her life experience and made it into one endless love story. When she's not writing or working on her MFA, she's singing loudly and off-key, hanging out with friends, or playing with her 2.5 fur babies. She can usually be found with a kiss in one hand and a twist of lime in the other, exactly the kind of stories she likes to read and write. If you'd like to know more about Brigit, you can find out more on her website.

BRIGITROSE.WORDPRESS.COM

OTHER WORKS BY BRIGIT ROSÉ

LOVE'S WORTH SERIES
UnHinged
ReIgnited

FAIRYTALE RETELLINGS
Grace's Beast

Under Krys Fenner

DARK ROAD SERIES
Addicted
Damaged
Avenged

THE GUARDHIAN SERIES
Awakened
Disillusioned

COMING SOON

Burned (Dark Road Series)
ReUnited (Love's Worth Series)